Two Wives
One Family

By Janette Grant

Mindworks Publishing

Dedicated to my mother, Sheila Lynne Grant,

The strongest, most beautiful woman to grace my life and one of the major reasons for writing this book. I love you and I never stop missing you.

Nothing functions by itself, I now realize. Everything is interrelated – body, mind and spirit. Family, community, country. Job, education, heritage, home. History, culture, religious beliefs, principles. How we put all these together in our lives makes up the unique individuals we are.

The Dancing Healers
Carl A. Hammerschlag, M.D.

Chapter One

Summer

My dandelion yellow khimar slides back over my brown, bald head and pools around my neck for the second time in the last fifteen minutes. I picked this scarf because it's so bright and pretty, but the silky chiffon has absolutely nothing to grip onto. Cancer and chemotherapy can do that to you. My hair started thinning and falling out a few weeks before starting chemo so I took the plunge and just shaved it all off. It wasn't easy. I admit that I was a little vain about my hair. Subhaana'Allah, Allah Ta'aala does everything for a reason.

I'm sitting in the doctor's office beside my husband, Michael, listening but not listening to what Dr. Alonzo, my oncologist, is saying. I lift the soft material back up and drape it over my head and shoulders, chastising myself for not using a hijab pin today. The air conditioning in the tidy office is up too high and I'm cold in the white and yellow cotton tunic of my shalwar kameez - the thin scarf doesn't provide much warmth. I should have brought a sweater.

"The tumors are gone, and everything looks good. Her weight is up, and she's got some energy back," I hear Dr. Alonzo say, speaking about me in the third person and talking more to Michael than to me. "I'd like her to undergo radiation treatments, however. Just to make sure that the cancer has completely gone into remission."

I tense at that suggestion, coming out of my emotional stupor long enough to recognize that they are about to make an important decision about my body without me. I look away from the bright blue sky that I'd been gazing at through the window and I shift my gaze to Michael's profile. As if sensing my alarm, he glances at me, his light brown eyes conveying that he understands, and reaches for my hand, holding it loosely in his as he responds. Michael and I had already talked about this at home: I don't want to go through the radiation treatments.

"About that," Michael says to the doctor. "She says she feels much better. She doesn't want to go through with the radiation treatments."

Dr. Alonzo frowns slightly and turns his attention to me. His brown eyes squint slightly with curiosity and his expression is bewildered. If I had to guess, I'd say he's around 55 years old and despite being a doctor, he's a little on the heavy side in terms of his weight. He has a grandfatherly way about him that has endeared him to our family throughout this whole ordeal, and I'm reluctant to disappoint him, but I've made up my mind. I sit up straighter in my chair and clear my throat nervously before I start.

"First I want to say thank you. Thank you for taking such good care of me and for helping me face the cancer, but I don't want to go through anymore procedures. I feel better overall, but after the last chemotherapy session I felt really sick and drained – like it's the chemo that's wearing me down now," I say, shifting uncomfortably in my chair.

My heart is racing in my chest and Dr. Alonzo's deepening frown only increases my anxiety, but I squeeze Michael's hand for strength and state firmly, "I don't want to go through with the radiation treatment. For the record, I'm refusing further treatment, but thank you for all that you've done for me."

Dr. Alonzo's eyes soften and his frown melts away when I finish. His voice is quiet when he speaks.

"Sounds like she's decided," he says softly, glancing over at Michael, his tone amused and slightly ironic. "I know when I can't budge a patient. At least promise me that you'll get a second opinion. I'm going to set up an appointment at the

Dana Farber Cancer Center in Boston for you. Will you do that for me?"

Dr. Alonzo looks directly at me when he asks this, and with sincere concern shining from his brown eyes as he waits for my response. I don't want to, but I cannot refuse him. A second opinion won't hurt. I'll just have to let that doctor know as well that I'm done. Three months of chemotherapy has been enough for me. The last round had me so sick that I thought I was dying. After making salat al-istikaarah, I decided to refuse further treatment and I am faithfully sticking to my decision, but I'll go for the second the opinion for Dr. Alonzo's sake.

I nod my head in response, and both Dr. Alonzo and Michael sigh with relief. This is the first sign to me that Michael doesn't want me to refuse the radiation treatment and his relief surprises me because he's been so verbally supportive about my decision. I push my surprise away and decide to wait until we leave the office before asking him about it. Dr. Alonzo picks up the phone on his desk to call the nurse in the reception area to set up the appointment. Michael smiles encouragingly at me, squeezing my hand.

There are circles under his eyes, but they crinkle at the corners with his smile and the circles only make me love him more. He stopped work to bring me to the appointment so he's wearing a light blue button-down shirt, a black kufi and dark grey slacks having left the matching suit jacket in the car. We've had enough worry and sleeplessness to last us a lifetime over the past six months. I was diagnosed with Non-Hodgkins Lymphoma, a cancer of the lymphatic system, in early February after nearly a year of sluggishness then noticing a lump in my groin. Life has been a roller coaster of emotions ever since. I'd be happy to never see another MRI machine or butterfly needle for the rest of my life!

Dr. Alonzo hangs up the phone and returns his full attention to us, standing from behind his desk and coming around it to shake Michael's hand and to give me a hug.

"Katie will give you the appointment slip for Dana Farber when you go out, and you take good care of her, ok?" Dr. Alonzo says to Michael as he shakes his hand before turning to me and hugging me around the shoulders.

"And you take care of yourself. You have to be around to take care of that precious little boy you have," he says to me.

My eyes well up with tears as gratitude overwhelms me. This kind, portly, Italian American doctor who I might never have had the opportunity to meet or to talk to if it hadn't been for the cancer that had invaded my body had carefully and compassionately walked with me through CAT scans, MRI scans, chemotherapy treatments, biopsies, fear of the unknown and debilitating pain. And now, here I stand, six months later, bald and without eyebrows, a little on the thin side, but stronger and better than I was when I had first walked into his office. To say thank you just simply doesn't feel like enough. I pray that Allah Ta'aala will reward him for all of the good and healing that he brought into my life. He pinches my cheek affectionately after the brief hug. I can tell that he understands my tears.

"All right. Get out of here you two," he says affectionately and goes back to his desk.

Michael grasps my hand and waves good-bye to him as we leave the office.

When we enter the brightly lit outer office the nurse/appointment setter, Katie, greets us with a smile. She hands Michael the appointment slip for the Dana Farber Center.

"Here you go," she says cheerfully. "And make sure you come back and see us – let us know how you're doing, ok?"

We nod and smile back at her as we exit the heavy glass doors leading out to the main lobby of the medical center. The early afternoon summer sunlight shines brightly through the windows of the lobby, and we cross the smooth tiled floor to wait for the automated doors to open. We are immediately struck with a blast of hot, humid air from outside when they do. I love it and I lift my face to the sun as it warms me, but Michael flinches as if he's been hit in the face. Clasping my hand tightly in his, he begins to hurry across the front facade of the hospital, and over towards the patient parking lot where his car is parked. I struggle to keep up with his long strides.

At 5 feet tall and wearing a new pair of sandals that haven't been broken in yet, I hope I don't slip as he, at 6'5 and long-legged, races towards the car and the cool promise of the air conditioning.

After about thirty seconds I let go of his hand, winded, and say, "You go ahead. I'll meet you there."

He stops immediately and looks down at me apologetically with concern.

"Are you ok? Sorry babe," he says and waits with me while I catch my breath.

I smile crookedly, mostly with embarrassment at having gotten winded so quickly. In this condition it's hard to believe that I had once been a high school competitor for the 100 meter dash; now I can hardly cross a parking lot at too brisk a pace or walk up too many stairs. I've never felt so physically and emotionally vulnerable before now. Sweat begins to gather on Michael's forehead while he waits for me.

"I'm sorry," I say as I catch my breath.

He shakes his head vehemently and replies, "No. Stop it. You don't have anything to be sorry about anything. You can wait here, and I'll go get the car."

He glances around and spots a bench, then takes his time walking with me over to it. It's in the shade of an old Maple tree beside the bus stop for taking patients to and from the medical center.

"I'll be right back," he says and kisses my forehead before turning and striding away towards the parking lot.

I try not to feel apologetic, but I can't help myself. He has taken on so much of the responsibilities around the house lately that I'm beginning to feel like a burden. Part of why I want to stop the chemo and not go any further with the radiation treatment is because I want to get back to my old self. I don't want to have to need help getting in and out of the bathtub, or to have to ask for someone to cook food for me. It's been incredibly humbling, which I'm thankful for, but I don't feel like much of a partner these days and I can't stop myself from feeling guilty about it.

Just then there's a break in the clouds and the sun shines through them as a soft breeze blows the leaves in the tree above me. In my mind it feels like a gentle hug from the Most High, assuring me that everything is going to be ok. I take a deep breath and look around the people walking in front of the medical center and the steady traffic on the street beyond the bus stop. I wonder what they might be going through in their lives and what challenges they may be facing, and I recognize the mercy of my circumstances.

Michael pulls up in front of the bench at that moment and I stand up to reach for the door to the passenger seat. I get in, putting on my mask of cheerful optimism as I climb in, careful to not reveal the leaning of my thoughts. I wear an emotional mask more often than not these days, I realize. I feel like I have to. Seeing the fear in my family's eyes when they look at me has become too much to bear in addition to my own fears, so I do my best to hide the fact that I'm struggling inside.

Hopefully now that the cancer is in remission and the treatments have ended that will change.

I look out the window at the green and rich brown colors of summer as we drive, praying that I've made the right decision. A still, silent voice within tells me that I have. I don't doubt that there will be challenges ahead, but I'm hopeful that things will get better. That I'll get better.

"That went good, I think," Michael says, making small talk as we drive past Rhode Island Hospital and towards downtown Providence. "He didn't try to talk you out of it. And a second opinion is a good idea."

He turns up the car's air conditioning as he speaks. His words yank me from the view outside the window and I remember his sigh of relief in the doctor's office.

"You seemed relieved when I agreed to that," I say, somewhat accusingly. "I thought you were with me in this. I thought you understood."

"I am with you, and I do understand," he replies hastily and glances over at me to stress his sincerity before returning his eyes to the road. "But it doesn't hurt to make sure that this is the best choice. The Dana Farber Center has a lot of specialists, maybe there's an alternative treatment available that won't be as hard on your body as the chemo has been. You were supposed to complete another round of chemo, remember? Let's just make sure everything is all good."

I shrug but I don't say anything, and I turn my head to look back out the window. I don't want to start a disagreement and I'm feeling like I might if I continue. He has supported my decision without objection, but there has been added tension since I made it. We drive along in silence for a few minutes before he speaks again.

"Are you hungry? We can stop somewhere to get something to eat before heading home," he says.

"No, I'm ok," I reply. "But if you're hungry I don't mind stopping."

He shakes his head negative and says, "No, I'm not really hungry either."

The silence becomes uncomfortable as we both retreat to our own thoughts. I can't imagine what he might be thinking but my own thoughts drift once again towards self-pity and feeling like a burden. He has started a new business recently and he's had to take time from work to drive me to the doctor's today, and although I had insisted that my mother was willing to bring me, he had refused. He hasn't ever said anything to make me feel like a burden, but we hardly talk anymore unless he's asking me about how I'm feeling or reminding me to eat or to take my medication or vitamins or to pray. Our relationship has been reduced to one more like a child being steered around in particular directions than to an equal partner in a marriage. At least that's how I've begun to feel.

It's a Wednesday afternoon in July but the traffic is bumper-to-bumper as we drive past Kennedy Plaza and towards Providence Place Mall. I deliberately turn my attention to the cars around us and I wonder what event might be happening nearby to cause such a back-up in traffic – anything to keep my mind off my emotions.

Not only have Michael and my parents been carrying the load of driving me back and forth from doctor's appointments, doing grocery shopping and all of the cooking around the house, and taking care of Gabey when I'm too tired; but I've also had to take time away from work during the busiest time of the year in our department at the university. The past five months have been the most difficult months of my life so far and that's saying a lot after having gone through the struggle of accepting the fact that Michael had married a second wife last year.

Thinking about Nicole, my co-wife, suddenly makes me even more uncomfortable as we drive in silence towards our neighborhood. She and I had initially been doing well when it came to getting along, but that was when she was living miles away in Massachusetts while I was living here in Rhode Island. Michael had been splitting his time equally between our two locations, so we didn't have much, if any, day-to-day interaction as co-wives. Now that she is living right next door, however, is a whole different experience. The honeymoon is definitely over, which makes me sad because we were once so close.

I guess it could just be me, but it seems like we're holding one another at arm's length, cautiously maneuvering around situations that might cause or reveal jealousy between us. As converts to Islam, polygyny is a new concept to both of us and we have all taken a leap of faith when it comes to living this lifestyle. It's only been a month since she moved to Rhode Island, and she and I started out making an effort to spend time with each other when Michael isn't around, but with me feeling tired most of the time from the chemo and her working during the day at a new, rigorous job, it's been a challenge. The last time she and I had been together it hadn't ended well. Michael had come home from work early and had stopped by to see me while Nicole was visiting and the air had become so thick with unexpressed emotions from all three of us that I had found it hard to breathe.

I hope and pray that things will get better between her and I and that the tension that I've felt between us won't start to affect my relationship with Michael . . . I push those thoughts out of my head, and I try to focus on the future and on getting healthy again. I give myself an internal pep talk, doing my best to convince my mind that now with the cancer in remission I can get back to living without fear and then everything will fall peacefully and blissfully back into place. I'll go back to work, I'll get back into the swing of taking care of my son Gabriel, and the moments of discomfort that have appeared between Michael, Nicole and I will disappear. Nicole and I won't treat one another so suspiciously, and all three of us can get back to the business of building our family. Yes. That's what I'm going to focus on this summer. Inshaa'Allah, with the help of Allah, I will be successful.

Michael has the air conditioning on blast, so I roll down my window a little, just enough to let in some warmth from outside. I allow my eyes to roam over the bright green lawn of the park by the elementary school then past a woman as she rides her bike over the bike trail beyond the lawn. I can hear the cheerful notes of a lemonade truck tinkling in the distance as the smell of burning charcoal seeps into the car.

Summer. I smile and surrender myself to optimism and the bright afternoon sunlight. The logo of a Dell's Lemonade truck catches my eye next as it passes in the traffic beside us, and I'm reminded of days spent at the beach and of backyard barbecues. Engulfed by the sights, sounds and scents of summer, I roll the window down a little more and I hope for the best.

Chapter Two

Home

We pull up to the little white and red duplex that we
share with Nicole and Michael parks his car on our
side of the driveway behind mine. I was
disappointed when we had to move out of our little
house on the East Side, but we simply hadn't been
able to afford it. Michael had found this duplex in
the Smith Hill area near Rhode Island College, and
he had been able to make a deal with the landlord
for a reduced price for renting both units which was
a blessing.

There's not as much space here as there had been in
the house on Elgin Street, and this two-story, two-
bedroom duplex is arranged more like a mini
apartment complex than a house (with its limited
storage and tiny closet space) but the neighborhood
is nice and peaceful, and there's a park for Gabey to
play in within walking distance. Nicole is still at
work, so her side of the driveway is empty. Michael
and I sit inside the coolness of the car for a few
silent moments before he turns to me expectantly.

"I should get back to the office," he says,
apologetically. "Those two investors I told you

about are stopping by today to take a look at the office space. I really need to be there.”

I’d completely forgotten about that.

“Oh yeah. Right,” I say and I reach for the car door handle.

“Will you be ok? How are you feeling? Do you want me to drop you off at your folks house?” he asks with his now customary concern.

“No, I’m fine. I’ll be fine. Aunt Pam will be dropping Gabey off in a few hours anyway, so I’ll call her if I need anything or if I start feeling sick,” I reply and I climb out of the car before leaning back in through the open door to kiss his cheek. “As salaamu Alaikum, hon.”

He smiles and replies, “Walaikum as salaam. I’ll be home around 6. Don’t forget to take your iron supplements and the nausea pills. And there’s leftover potato and carrot soup in the fridge.”

“Ok,” I say, still wearing my mask, and I smile back as I close the car door.

He keeps the car idling in the driveway as I walk over to the front of the duplex and reach into my purse for my house keys. Once I’ve opened the front door, I turn back and wave, letting him know that I’m in. He honks the horn to acknowledge my wave and begins backing out of the driveway as I close the door.

Once inside, I put my keys back into my purse before hanging it on the coat rack by the door, then I remove my sandals and place them on the low shoe shelf beneath the rack. I chide myself internally for the irritation that I'm feeling about his reminders. It's cool inside even though I had turned off the air conditioning before we had left for the appointment, so I keep my scarf draped over my head and shoulders as I walk around the small living room to open up the windows and let in a little warmth from outside. There's an old Maple tree on the sidewalk in front of one of the windows with a bird's nest high in its branches and as soon as I open the window, I can hear the birds chirping.

The sound of the birds makes me smile and relax my shoulders. One of the main lessons that I've learned during this illness is how my body never lies, even if my mind might try to hide what it's feeling, and at the moment, I'm frustrated and annoyed. I drop into the armchair by the window and take a deep breath before exhaling slowly. Leaning my head against the back of the chair, I tune into what's really happening inside of me body and I close my eyes.

I know Michael only reminds me about the medication and eating right because he loves me, and I know that it's ungrateful for me to react this way, but I can't ignore or deny what I'm feeling. I compare our recent conversations to the conversations that we used to have, and I feel a sense of loss. We used to talk about books, and politics, about religion and philosophy. Now we talk about how much I've eaten or slept, or about my next doctor's appointment or most recent test results. My mind wanders towards imagining what he and Nicole talk about and I feel the icy shards of jealousy spread over my heart.

As I sit, the dream that I had last night arises in my mind. In the dream I was upset about a suspicion that I had about Nicole's intentions towards me, so I knocked on her door to confront her and to ask her about it. She opened the door and looked at me with a flat expression, but she didn't say anything. I demanded that she tell me what was going in with her, but she refused and said that she didn't have to tell me anything and slammed the door in my face.

I had woken up in a sweat and my heart had been racing with rage at her response. I was so disturbed that I had been ready to bolt out of the bed and to go over to her unit, but I could hear my two-year-old son Gabey crying in his bedroom, so I had forgotten all about the dream and had instead gone to take care of him. He was standing up in his crib, clutching at the wooden rails with tears streaming down his little round face. I fell asleep with him laying on my chest as I rocked him in our rocking chair, and I hadn't thought about the dream again until this moment.

Thinking about it now, the rage has dwindled from an all-out flaming fireball to smokey simmering coals, but it remains. I feel my shoulders tense up again and a knot forms in my stomach as I replay the dream in my mind, trying to analyze the symbols to find meaning. I admit to myself that I feel threatened by Nicole's proximity and her living so close; like she can affect how Michael feels about me and possibly absorb all of his affection and attention. Especially now.

I admit to myself that I don't feel very confident or self-assured these days. The cancer and chemotherapy treatments have left me frail, mentally, spiritually and physically. And to add to the physical frailty, I'm essentially hairless from my bald head to my non-existent leg hair. I remember distinctly the day when I first noticed the hair crumbling and rolling off my arms in the shower as I washed up and how much it had freaked me out. Although I don't miss the thin layer of hair on my face and chin (telltale evidence of my Cape Verdean heritage on my mother's side) I feel naked and

vulnerable without the thick curly mass of my hair.
It had been halfway down my back when it had
started falling out. My mother had bought me a
beautiful black wig, similar in style and texture to
my own hair, but it was itchy and way too hot to
wear under my hijab, especially now that it's
summer.

And I have always been petite, but I look at myself
now in the mirror and I cringe. My usually vibrant
chocolate brown complexion is ashen, my arms and
legs are thin, and my figure looks more like that of a
pre-adolescent girl than that of a 24-year-old
mother. I've started to regain some weight and I
weighed in at 105 lbs at my appointment today, but
that's 20 lbs less than my average.

In addition to the physical changes in my body, I've
also been enveloped by a mental fog, and I have
been too tired to keep up with my five daily prayers.
As a result, my spiritual connection with Allah feels
weaker than it has been in the past. Islam teaches
that illness is an opportunity to receive forgiveness
from Allah and that going through a serious illness
achieves mercy and forgiveness of sins, but I'm
ashamed to admit that at this point, I'm just trying
to remain in gratitude that the worst seems to be
over. Seeing Nicole with her shining skin and bright
eyes – the image of good health and vitality – only
makes me feel even more insecure about myself.

To Nicole's credit, she hasn't done or said anything to make me feel this way, but we hardly ever talk anymore either so it's hard to know much of anything concerning how she feels. Most of our conversations center around coordinating our household expenses which is another disappointment. We met during our first year of college and had hit it off immediately. She and I had actually met before either of us had met Michael. We were both communications majors, we enjoyed most of the same music and movies, and we were a lot alike when it came to how we viewed life and our roles as women of color in the world. We had even discovered Islam around the same time and had taken our shahadah within months of each other.

During college, she had become one of my closest friends. I still consider her to be one of the closest people to me, so much so that when I first received the news about the cancer diagnosis, and I was faced with the extremely difficult task of accepting what that meant – possible death - it had been comforting to know that Michael and Gabriel would have Nicole in their lives if I didn't survive. I still feel that way, but now, with the cancer in remission, I have to face the challenge of *living* with the reality of the love and affection that my husband and my son have for her without falling down the rabbit hole of jealousy, insecurity, and self-sabotage.

I sit and re-evaluate the relationships between the three of us and the shared goals that we have started this family with. Our faith in God is the motivation and it is the glue that holds us together. By Allah's grace I've survived the cancer and the chemotherapy treatments, and I hold on to the belief that it will be by Allah's grace that our family will also survive and thrive as we enter into this next level of development.

As I sit here thinking, I realize that the dream is warning me. There may be something that Nicole is feeling that she doesn't want to share with me, and I think I should accept that fact, no matter how angry I may feel about it. She doesn't have to tell me everything that is on her mind any more than I have to tell her everything that is on mine. I also realize that I don't want to go knocking on any doors that might have anything behind it that I may not be emotionally able to handle. The Qur'an says that suspicion in some cases is a sin, and when I interpret my feelings in the dream, my reaction was to a suspicion in my heart about her, not from any particular action taken or words spoken by her. I don't want to take any chances of possibly committing a sin, but at the same time I also cannot ignore my intuition. I accept the dream for the warning that I believe it is and I decide to keep moving forward; I decide to let go of the rage and to pray for a peaceful solution to whatever may be lurking behind closed doors.

I breathe easier knowing that I can choose to do better to relax when it comes to her and I. There may be an increasing lack of stable, common ground when she and I try to talk to one another lately, but our home is supposed to be an abode of peace, so I have to do my part to keep it that way, even if I'm not feeling very peaceful these days. I have to try to react differently to situations when they arise.

Feeling better and like I have a thread of light to follow, I open my eyes and I get up to go into the kitchen to make a cup of coffee. The time on the clock on the microwave says 2:41pm in neon green. My Aunt Pam, my mother's older sister, has been helping out with taking care of my son during the day when I have a doctor's appointment and she will be arriving in about an hour to bring Gabey home. Taking advantage of the free time, and the fact that I'm not nauseous or exhausted today, I pour spring water from the gallon we leave on the countertop into the glass pot of the coffee maker, and I slide it onto the burner of the coffee maker so I can fill the filter. I place a paper filter inside and I scoop out enough ground coffee to make the minimum amount before inserting, then I turn the coffee maker on.

The smooth aroma begins to fill the kitchen and I take a look in the refrigerator for a snack to have with it. There's one more slice of cheese Danish left! I slide container of leftover potato and carrot soup to the side, and I carry the Danish and the coffee creamer back over to the counter. I get a plate and a mug from the cabinet and once the coffee is finished brewing and I've sugared and creamed my coffee cup to perfection, I bring it and the plate of Danish outside to the little back porch off the kitchen where we've set up a small grill, a little potted lemon tree, and a card table with three chairs.

The patio is split down the middle by a pretty, slatted wooden fence to separate this side of the duplex from Nicole's side, and there's an awning overhead to deflect the sun and the rain so it's one of my favorite spots to relax. There's a common patch of grass below the patios and although we haven't spent any time together as a family back here yet, hopefully we will before the summer is over.

I turn on the radio/cd player combo that I have set up on the center of the table and I skip to one of my favorite Stevie Wonder songs, *Overjoyed*, from his

In Square Circle album. I let Stevie serenade me as I focus on the future and try to visualize the best outcomes in the days and weeks ahead.

Chapter Three

Back to Life

"Are you sure you're ok? Do you want something to drink: some water or tea?" my manager Carol asks.

Her light gray eyes are filled with empathy as she follows me to the refrigerator in the conference room where I deposit my lunch. It's my first day back to work at the university and although I'm excited to get back to it, not everyone in the office seems to agree with me. It's been less than a month since my last session of chemotherapy and despite the fact that I'm 5lbs shy of my normal 125lbs, *and* the fact that I'm nausea free, my eyebrows are growing back, and there's a light fluff of curly black hair on my head beneath my hijab, two out of three of my co-workers think that I need at least another month at home to fully get my strength back.

Middle-aged and soft spoken, Carol, the Department Manager, has been more like a doting aunt than a supervisor in the two years since I've been working here. Aaron, a grad student and the Center's in house Research Assistant, meets us in the hallway as Carol follows me out of the conference room and into my office across the way. They both stop to hover around my desk with watchful expressions as I take off my sweater and drape it over my chair. It's a bright, August morning but the air conditioning in the building is wintery so I made sure I came prepared with a sweater today.

"How are you feeling?" Aaron asks quietly with the all-too-familiar expression of concern and sympathy on his face.

I adjust my emotional mask and smile cheerfully and reply, "I'm feeling great! Almost back to normal."

He and Carol exchange a discreet look of doubt.

"Really. I don't need anything at all other than to get back to work," I say emphatically as I sit down at my desk and look up eagerly at them.

Carol eyes me for a moment, with indecision written all over her face, before stepping away from my desk and replying, "Ok. But for the record, I think you should wait until September to come back so I'll be watching you closely."

"Fair enough and duly noted," I respond with a smile. "You sound so much like my mother that it makes me wonder if you two have been talking.

And don't be surprised if she pops up randomly here at the Center for the next few weeks."

Carol laughs and says, "She and I haven't spoken but I can just imagine how she must feel, and I don't doubt for a minute that she'll be crossing campus to come over here to check on you."

My mother, Lynne Burrows, also works at the university as a senior administrative secretary in the Africana Studies Department. She has never admitted to helping me get this job at the Center for the Study of Race and Ethnicity but I'm sure that she had a hand in it.

Just then, Shayleene Marrow, the Director of the Center, enters the office and smiles brightly, filling the room with her presence. She's also a Professor in the Education Department and one of the few African American female professors at the university. Needless to say, she's a force and has been a mentor. Her smooth brown skin is glowing and as always, she is dressed impeccably. She is the only one of our small staff that thinks it's a good idea for me to be back at work.

"It's so good to see you!" she says and comes around the desk to give me a hug. "We're so glad to have you back! How do you like the new computer?"

They've replaced the old bulky Dell PC that I used to work on with a smooth, sleek Macintosh.

"I love it!" I answer honestly. "I can't wait to get familiar with it."

"Good," she says and turns to exit the office. "I have a few things to do and a quick meeting this morning, then I'll be taking the day off, but you let Carol know if you need anything at all."

"I will. Thank you, Shayleene," I reply.

Once Shayleene is gone Carol sighs, caving under Shayleene's enthusiasm, and smiles before saying, "Well. There really isn't much to do around here. The high school kids have finished the summer program, and the undergrads haven't come back to campus yet, so it's been pretty slow. Why don't you check the phone messages and emails for now, then setup your accounts and course files on the new computer."

"Ok," I say, relieved that she's giving me space to get back to work.

The Center for the Study of Race and Ethnicity in America is one of the newer departments established here at Brown University and I am blessed to have been hired as the department secretary. It's not quite what I'd had in mind for a dream job after studying Journalism in college and interning at the local newspaper, but my co-workers are great, the benefits are amazing, it helps pay the bills, and I have the option of finishing my bachelor's degree here with reduced tuition costs for employees. I didn't quite appreciate the value of an ivy league degree as a senior in high school, but after two years of marriage and taking a leave of absence from college, I sure do now.

Carol and Aaron smile and leave before going back to their respective offices: hers is across from mine and his is further down the hall. Once I'm alone, I open the deep bottom left hand drawer of my desk to store my purse and my work bag, then I take my cellphone from my purse and put it beside my elbow on the desk before closing the drawer and booting up the shiny new computer.

And I really do love it. It's like getting a new car! The operating system is so much faster than my old Dell that I spend an hour setting up the new email, word processing, and spreadsheet programs without realizing that so much time had passed. I'm just getting started transferring course information that I've emailed to myself to new files on the computer when I hear the front door alarm chime as the main door is opened.

Many of the buildings on campus are old colonials and have large rooms with high ceilings so it's hard to hear if someone is entering. Our building, like many of the others, use an alarm system to notify the staff when someone enters and exits. I look up from my desk as I hear footsteps approaching my office which is also the general reception area.

"Hey!" Joshua Olivera cries out in surprise when he recognizes me. "Small world! I didn't know you work here."

My mouth opens with surprise of my own and I fumble for words as he enters my office and stands in front of my desk to greet me. I haven't seen him in months and the sight of him is so unexpected that I'm at a loss for words. We went to the same high school back in the day and I, like so many of my female classmates, had a HUGE crush on the then high school basketball star. Seeing him again this way is sort of like having a local celebrity step into my office.

"How have you been? I haven't forgotten how you and your girls did me that night the last time I saw you when you all had that Chinese food, by the way," he says conversationally with a friendly smile.

He's still very handsome to look at despite the years that have passed since high school, and I begin to feel self-conscious. I recall the instance that he is talking about from a few months ago with amusement. He lives across the street from my best friend, Lisa, and he had tried to get us to give him some of the Chinese food that we had bought for dinner one night.

I laugh at the memory of Lisa closing the door in his face, feeling a little guilty, and I respond, "That was all Lisa. It's her house. But I admit, we didn't really want to share. I'm good. How are you?"

"Good. Good," he says, his brown eyes bright with genuine pleasure. "I'm here for a meeting with the Director. I run a non-profit and we've qualified for a grant from the Center."

"Nice," I reply, surprised and impressed. "Congratulations. I'll just let Shayleene know that you're here."

I pick up my desk phone and dial the extension to Shayleene's office to let her know that Joshua has arrived. She tells me to send him in and we hang up.

"She's expecting you," I say and come around from behind my desk to walk him out into the corridor so I can show him the way to Shayleene's office.

"Ok. Thanks," he says as he follows me.

We step out into the corridor, and I turn around too quickly, almost bumping into him.

"Sorry. Her office is right there," I say and point to the open door on the right, directly next to my office. "You can go on in."

"Thank you. I'll stop by to chat for a minute on my way out if you're not busy," he says but it's more of a question than a statement.

"Sure," I say, flattered and more self-conscious.

He smiles and nods and turns away to walk the few feet required to reach Shayleene's office. I return to my desk, pleasantly surprised at his appearance and still smiling. The last time we'd seen each other was almost a year ago, but we had graduated from high school together nearly seven years before that, and the East Side of Providence, Rhode Island is a small, close-knit community where almost everybody knows each other from growing up in the public and private schools in the neighborhood. Especially among the people of color. Even before high school we had known about each other – well, my friends and I had known about him anyway.

As pre-adolescent girls often do, we had crushes on several of the boys around the neighborhood and he was one of the universally good-looking ones that *everyone* had a crush on from about 6th grade and up. It embarrasses me to think about it now, but we actually used to ride past his house on our bikes and call out his name before disappearing around the corner and out of sight. He questioned us about it once during high school, but we denied it of course. High school was years away from 6th grade, however, and there were moments when I'd imagined myself going out on a date with him as a 10th grader, but those were fantasies restricted to confidential conversations at sleepovers and prohibited from ever being spoken of in the light of day.

It was great to see him now, and to know that he had done well for himself, and if I remember correctly, I think he might have stated that he had played basketball overseas in a predominantly Muslim country while in college.

I go back to my desk and I continue organizing computer files and setting up new folders for the upcoming academic year. I may have left college myself after two years of study but being in this environment keeps the fire of the pursuit of knowledge burning within me so the work is welcome and often educational. Working on a college campus has its pros and cons, but I can't imagine working anyplace else. The regular lectures and the campus wide symposiums constantly inspire my curiosity and I'm looking forward to checking out the events calendar for the upcoming fall semester.

By the time I finish setting up the files it's 10:45am and I'm starting to feel hungry which is a great sign. Overall my energy levels are good but I sometimes lose my appetite and get tired in the afternoons. I get up to walk across the corridor to the conference room where I've got a cucumber and melon smoothie in my lunch bag, but before I can step across the threshold Shayleene and Joshua come out of her office and stop me.

"Joanna! You should have said that you two went to high school together! What a delight! He and I were talking and since you're back, would you be up to attending the basketball tournament that his non-profit is organizing and taking some pictures for the Center's newsletter? This would be a great feature for our annual report," Shayleene says with excitement written all over her face and I can almost see the gears churning in her brilliant mind. "Hopefully Aaron can go with you and make some community connections with some of the other organizers. This could really put the Center where it needs to be in the heart of the community."

Joshua is grinning from ear to ear and looking at me expectantly. One of Shayleene's prime objectives since becoming the Director has been to add more of a neighborhood-based community activist component to the otherwise academic focus of the Center's programs and she persuasively pushes her message to anyone who will listen. She has obviously worked her magic on him and has gotten him to agree with this idea.

"Sure," I respond, somewhat hesitantly. "When is it?"

And I'm hesitant not because of the idea itself, but because of emotions that the idea of going to his event has stirred up in me.

"At the end of the month. It's a back-to-school tournament to get the kids excited about the coming school year. We'll be giving out free school supplies and setting up booths for small businesses and community organizers," Joshua says.

"I'll leave you two to sort out the details," Shayleene says with a smile and returns to her office.

Joshua and I look at each other expectantly for a few seconds, him waiting for me to respond to his last statement, and me indecisive about whether to make an excuse so I can go get my smoothie or to wait and talk with him first. My body decides that it doesn't want to wait so I make my mind and body compromise.

"I was just about to take a quick break," I say and gesture towards the conference room. "Can we talk in here?"

"Yes. Of course. Wherever," he says and follows me into the brightly lit, carpeted space.

I suddenly feel like I'm back in high school and being paid attention to by the most popular guy in school as I lead the way. He sits down at the conference table in the center of the room while I make a quick detour to the refrigerator for my smoothie.

"Would you like some coffee? Or tea? We have bottled water also, if you prefer," I say, concealing my nervousness, and I stop by the table against the wall beside the refrigerator where our in-house coffee station is setup.

"No, I'm fine. Thank you," he replies comfortably.

I sit across from him at the conference table and twist open the top of my thermal tumbler, forcing myself to relax. I'm an adult now. I should not feel this uneasy. I take a swallow from the smoothie to settle my rumbling stomach.

"I apologize. My body has a mind of its own these days," I say in explanation.

"It's ok. No need to apologize. Lisa said that you're recovering from cancer and chemotherapy treatment. You look great. I'm glad that you're feeling better," he says and grins before continuing. "Yeah. I've been asking about you. Every time I ask, she mentions that you're married and that you have a kid, like I'm some kind of creep, but you know her: always looking out for her girl."

We laugh at that together, but I'm surprised and flattered to learn that he's been asking about me.

"Thank you. And yes. 5th grade started this friendship and we're more like sisters than friends, so the protectiveness is mutually intense," I say before changing the subject. "The tournament sounds great, though. Where will it be held?"

"At the Billy Taylor park, if whether permits. Otherwise, we'll have it in the Nathaniel Greene gymnasium and auditorium," he says. "I'm glad you're coming. Tell your people about it. Everything is free except for the tickets to the basketball game; we need to raise money for basketball uniforms for the kids."

"Wow. So, you run a non-profit?" I ask and take another drink from my smoothie, all nervousness subsiding as we ease into the conversation.

"Yeah. For about a year now. I've been coaching at RIC since I got back to the states two years ago. I got injured playing ball, and I was offered a job as the executive director at Black Boys Matter by a family friend," he says, rubbing his knee subconsciously.

"I'm sorry to hear about the injury. But executive director is not a loss. I've heard of Black Boys Matter. Congratulations again, that's great. You all work with at-risk boys in communities where there tends to be a lot of gang violence, right?" I ask, completely drawn in.

"Yes," he responds enthusiastically. "Our main office is downtown, but we have a small space over on Hope Street and another one across town on Broad Street."

"That's wonderful. Mashaa'Allah," I say, and 'mashaa'Allah' comes out instinctively so I hurry to explain. "That means 'this is what God wills,' it's an Arabic phrase that we say in Islam; a way of praising God for things that happen, especially good things."

"Yes, I know. I lived in the Emirates for a year during college playing basketball. It's a beautiful country. Beautiful people. And a beautiful religion," he says, and his expression changes to reflect curiosity. "I was shocked, but then again not shocked, to see that you've become Muslim. How did that happen?"

He leans forward and appears to be genuinely interested. I take another swallow from my smoothie and I consider what to say. I've found that there's no simple, one way to answer a question like this and the process of "converting" to Islam is ongoing so it's not as if it's a done deal, but not everyone is open to hearing that or able to understand it. I get the feeling, however, that he might be.

"Well," I begin and smile ruefully. "It's still happening, so it's hard to answer that. I still consider myself 'becoming' Muslim every day because every day I have to make the effort to submit to God more and more. To put it simply, reading an English translation of the Qur'an for the first time is what made me want to take shahadah so that was a major starting point for me. Do you know what the shahadah is?"

"Yes. I've learned a little bit about Islam, mostly while I was in the Emirates. I considered taking my own shahadah once or twice, but the rules of Islam were a lot for me to consider back when I was in college," he says sheepishly. "I've never read the Qur'an, but I've heard it recited in Arabic. It made me want to cry, I had to fight back tears. It's so beautiful."

I smile empathetically and with repressed emotion of my own. He's describing an experience that I have felt many times, and which humbles me whenever it happens. I know exactly what he means.

I nod and respond, "I know what you mean. It makes me cry to hear it in Arabic too sometimes. You should read it. When you understand some of what is being said, even if it's an English translation, it's transformative."

"Wow. Amazing," he says, smiling, and looking at me with an awestruck expression that gives me pause.

I look away and finish the rest of my smoothie. It's not as if he's staring at me, but I feel uncomfortable and I suddenly wish that Shayleene was here in the room with us. I could be wrong, but he seems a little more interested in me than in what I'm saying, and I realize that deep down, that pleases me. When

I put the tumbler down and glance back over at him, he clears his throat and appears to be embarrassed.

"I should get going and let you get back to work," he says and stands up from his seat at the table. "It's been nice talking to you. Maybe we can have lunch one day or something?"

An alarm sounds off in my head and I begin to feel guilty. I immediately back step. I must have sounded too eager during our conversation.

"Yes, it's been nice," I agree, standing as well. "I don't know about lunch, but I'll ask my husband about having you over for dinner one day. He has studied a lot about Islam. I think the two of you might hit it off."

His eyes widen with surprise and his expression morphs between doubt and discomfort before he smiles and says, "Maybe. Can I have your email address? I'll email you the details about the tournament, and we can keep in touch."

"Ok, sure," I reply, but I feel reluctant.

He pulls out a pen and a business card holder from his briefcase and hands the pen and a business card to me.

"Here. You can write your email on this," he says.

I write my work email address on the back of the card and hand it and the pen back to him. He smiles and accepts it before pulling out a second hard and handing it to me.

"All of my information is there," he says and looks as if he is about to give me a hug but reconsiders. "I'll be in touch. You take care."

"Thank you, and you too," I reply.

He smiles and waves good-bye before exiting the conference room and surprising me by saying, "As salaamu Alaikum."

I smile back widely and reply, "Walaikum as salaam."

Day one back to work and I feel like I've accomplished more than just earning an income – I've shared information about Islam with another human being which is priceless. I cannot, however, ignore the personal happiness that I feel after that little talk and that worries me. I push the worry aside and I tell myself that it was just nostalgia.

Sure it was, I hear a little voice in my head say, but I ignore that too.

Chapter Four

Adulthood

"That's why you need to lay off that pork," my younger brother James teases my father as we sit around the dinner table at my parents' house. "I bet your blood pressure is so high because you have to have that bacon with your breakfast every morning."

My mother, Michael and I hide our amusement behind our dinner glasses as we drink our juice to avoid eye contact and my father's irritation at that comment, but my little sister Jasmine laughs out right as my father mumbles and stutters angrily while trying to think of a sly comeback.

"I hope you don't think your blood pressure is any better. You've been eating that bacon right along with me every morning up until what, a few weeks ago when you decided to become a Muslim," my father finally manages to retort then laughs at his own cleverness and looks around the table with an expression full of confidence that he has efficiently avenged himself from my brother's teasing.

"I'm twenty years younger than you so my blood pressure is fine, praise be to Allah," James responds with a chuckle. "You on the other hand have what – thirty something years of clean-up work to do?"

Michael, Gabey and I are at my parents' house for Sunday dinner and as usual, we cannot get through the meal without my father, James and Michael cracking jokes. My father had been complaining about the lack of salt in my mother's lasagna and she had apathetically announced that my father wasn't getting any more salt then she informed us that his doctor had said that he has high blood pressure.

"So, what else did the doctor say?" I ask, diverting the conversation. "Do you have to start taking blood pressure medication, dad?"

My father, Joseph, swallows a mouthful of lasagna and says, "No. Not right now and hopefully I won't have to. He said I'm still young enough to catch it if I alter what I eat and exercise more. Ya' hear that youngin'?"

The last remark is aimed at James who grins and says, "All right, I hear you, old man. Then you need to come to campus one of these weekends and join me at track practice. I'll make sure you get some real exercise, youngin' style."

Everybody laughs at James' come-back, even my father, and my mother leans over to pat my father on the back playfully.

"If he can keep up. So, tonight he's going to have to eat the lasagna as it is," my mother adds with a chastising glance at my dad.

"Hmmm," my father grumbles lowly under his breath but he's still smiling and doesn't say anything in response as he scoops another forkful of lasagna into his mouth.

"That was delicious as usual," Michael says to my mother as he pushes his empty plate forward and leans back contentedly in his chair. "That's one of my favorites."

"Thank you, son-in-law," my mother beams as she replies, feeling vindicated after my father's remark about the lack of salt. "Where's Nicole tonight? I thought she was coming too?"

I freeze inadvertently and Michael and I look at each other briefly before Michael replies, "She has to work late. She has a deadline for one of her projects and has to have all of the animation done before the morning."

I mentally adjust the mask that I've been wearing for the past few months hoping that my parents won't sense that anything is amiss with me. Things haven't gotten better between Nicole and I, but they also haven't gotten any worse. We seem to have gotten stuck in a space where we simply co-exist politely with one another.

"Oh. Ok. Well, make sure you bring a plate home for her, Jo," my mother says to me. "And a piece of pie too. I know she loves my sweet potato pie."

"Yes, she sure does. I will," I say to my mother, and I divert attention from myself by taking Gabey's plate away from him before he can smear any more tomato sauce around on the tray of his highchair.

"Look at my baby!" I say with exasperation.

One of his new habits is playing with his food after he gets full. Everybody looks and laughs as he grins happily in response to the laughter. He's an absolute mess. He has pasta sauce all over his face and hands, and he even has a leaf of romaine lettuce in his curly black hair.

"My grandson enjoyed his Nana's lasagna too, I see," my mother says and laughs as she gets up from the table and goes over to the diaper bag not too far away on the hallway chair where she retrieves his baby wipes.

I'm thankful for the distraction that Gabriel has provided because my overly astute mother can always sense when something is going on with me, and the mention of Nicole made me get tense. Over the past three weeks since I've gone back to work, Nicole and I have grown further apart, and I'm still having troubling dreams about it. Granted, she has been working late at work on a new animated television series almost every night so by the time she gets in I'm usually in bed already, but neither of us have been making any efforts to nurture our friendship and it's beginning to affect me big time. We've talked face to face maybe twice since I've stopped having the chemotherapy treatments. I've now found myself trying to avoid seeing her or talking about her because of the mixed emotions that I've been feeling.

I clear away the empty plates and cups from the table while my mother cleans Gabey's face and hands, and I start rinsing dishes and loading them into the dishwasher. My father, Michael and James start talking about football and speculating about which teams will likely do well this season and my little sister Jasmine joins me at the sink with more dishes to rinse.

"What was that face about?" she asks in a whisper and takes over loading the dishwasher while I rinse and hand dishes to her. "You looked like you were about to panic when Ma asked about Nicole."

I shoot a quieting glance at her before checking to see if my mother has heard her, but my mother is completely enthralled by her grandson and isn't paying us any attention. I should have known that my mother's "mini-me" would see my reaction and check me on it. She's only fourteen but we have a running family joke that she's fourteen going on forty.

"What do you mean?" I say with denial. "I didn't make a face."

"Uh – yes you did," she presses me on it quietly. "I was looking right at you."

She can be even more stubborn than my mother sometimes, especially when she is worried about someone in the family.

"I'll tell you later," I whisper hurriedly as my mother joins us at the sink with Gabriel in one arm and his tray from his highchair in her free hand.

She hands me the tray so I can wash it off and says, "Thank you, my girls."

She's thanking us for loading the dishwasher and hasn't apparently heard anything that we were talking about.

"No problem, mama," I say, trying to keep my cool and eyeing Jasmine to make sure that she doesn't give anything away.

She doesn't and replies, "Welcome, mommy."

"Jo, will you get the pie and ice cream for everybody when you finish, and put on a pot of coffee," my mother asks before turning and walking towards the living room. "Me and my Gabey are gonna go make something with the blocks, right my baby?"

"Wight," Gabey agrees with his lisp that converts "r's" into "w's", making us all smile.

"Ok, mommy, I will. And you don't want any ice cream, right?" I ask her as she walks away.

"Right. Just pie and coffee," she replies.

Once she's gone Jasmine turns her full attention on me with a stare that is clearly threatening me to spill the beans about what is going on with me and Nicole. I discreetly gesture with my eyes towards the table where dad, Michael and James are still sitting and talking as I finish wiping off Gabey's tray.

"After we give them dessert," I say quietly.

She nods conspiratorially and takes the clean tray from me so she can re-attach it to the highchair. I go over to the countertop on the opposite side of the kitchen where the coffee pot and other appliances are to start on the coffee. Jasmine finishes loading the dishwasher and turns it on before getting a set of dessert plates from the cabinet and spoons from the drawer. She brings them over to me as the coffee pot starts gurgling and filling the kitchen with its aroma. I reach for the two sweet potato pies that my mother has left cooling on the opposite counter.

I cut slices of the pie and dish it onto the plates for everyone while Jasmine scoops out ice cream and James, as if drawn to the pie magnetically (my mother's sweet potato pie is his favorite dessert) joins us at the counter, smacking his lips loudly in Jasmine's ear to get a rise out of her. He is successful and receives an elbow to the stomach for it. He's nineteen years old but a big kid at heart, like our father.

"Hey! That hurt," he complains and takes the plate with the biggest slice of pie on it.

"I hate when you do that!" Jasmine states angrily and unapologetically.

James disappears into the living room where my father has already tuned the tv to one of his favorite sitcoms. Michael joins Jasmine and I at the kitchen counter and smiles down at us, rubbing his hands together hungrily as his gaze shifts to the pie.

"Which one is mine?" he asks eagerly.

Things have been strained between me and Michael lately too, but being at my parents' house always makes it easier for us to put aside our differences. They keep us focused on the goal which is the building up of our family.

"This one," I say, pointing to the plate on the left. "Do you want coffee?"

"Yes, please, and thank you ma'am," he says playfully before he picks up his plate and kisses the top of my head.

He nudges Jasmine's shoulder affectionately before joining the rest of the family in the living room, leaving me and Jasmine alone for the moment.

"Everything looks fine with you two," Jasmine says observantly with a quizzical expression. "What's going on?"

"Bring this to dad and mom first then I'll tell you," I whisper.

She sighs impatiently but picks up the plates for mom and dad and hurries into the living room.

She's right, for the most part. I can say that things are ok with Michael and I, but the easy way that we used to be able to express ourselves with each other is beginning to fade. Most of our interactions take effort these days, at least for my part. And I may not be able to read his mind, but I know him, and he definitely seems to be struggling with something internally, but he hasn't said what.

Jasmine comes back just as I finish adding sugar and creamer to mom and Michael's cups of coffee. I hold the cups out towards her with a mischievous grin and she sighs impatiently again before taking them and turning around to go back to the living room. When she comes back this time I have her and my plate ready and I motion for her to join me in the backyard where we can talk.

The sky is colored in streaks of pink, orange and lavender when we step through the creaky screen door and into the backyard. There's a warm breeze carrying the scent of lilacs and damp grass as the evening cools, and we sit down in two of the folding chairs at the patio table. Jasmine spoons pie and ice cream into her mouth but her eyes are glued to my face with anticipation. She's only fourteen so there's only so much that I can say to her, and I'm conscious of the impression that my words may have. She and most of my family have accepted the polygynous lifestyle that Michael, Nicole and I have adopted, but no one really understands it so I always tread lightly when talking about it.

"Well. First of all, nothing is 'going on'" I tell her candidly with a smile to reassure her. "Nicole and I just haven't been able to spend much time together lately and I feel a little sad about that."

It's a revelation to me as I speak the words out loud. That fact really is at the heart of all of the anxiety that I've been experiencing. I feel sad that we don't hang out anymore or laugh together, or pray together like we used to. It hurts to think about the many weekends and afternoons that I'd spent recuperating from chemotherapy without her there to hold my hand or to give me an encouraging word.

There's also the insecurity that I feel about my relationship with Michael as a result of the distance between the three of us, and the sting of jealousy that rears its head from time to time when she and Michael spend time together without me, but I'll never burden my fourteen-year-old baby sister with that information, at least not at such a tender age. And fortunately, she's still young enough to not have a clue about that – at least she doesn't appear to. She nods at me with understanding and her brown eyes soften with empathy.

"I know how that can feel. Trish and I don't spend that much time together anymore either. You should come over here more," she says compassionately. "We can hang out together and watch movies like we used to before you got sick."

Trish and Jasmine have been friends since pre-school and it bothers me to hear this, but it also makes tears prick at the back of my eyes in reaction to my sister's tenderness. I blink them away and smile gratefully at her.

"You are just the sweetest, you know that?" I say and lean over to kiss her cheek. "And I will. That sounds like a good idea. Exactly what I need."

She smiles happily and eats another spoonful of pie and ice cream, satisfied that she has solved that problem for me so quickly and easily. I smile too, and we look out at the evening sky together in a comfortable silence, but my smile is bittersweet. If only it were that simple of a solution. I feel the weight of adulthood collapsing onto my shoulders all of a sudden. I scoop up some of my own pie and ice cream and spoon it into my mouth.

Maybe all of these emotions that I've been feeling lately stem simply from missing my friend, but I have no idea of how to go about admitting that to Nicole or to anyone else. I wasn't even able to admit it to myself until I was forced to speak honestly to my baby sister in a way that wouldn't negatively affect her perception of Nicole, or her perception of Islam and the practice of polygyny. So much of what I have come to accept as "womanhood" revolves around being strong, independent, self-sufficient and bold, but I'm feeling incredibly vulnerable and insecure lately and it's starting to pull me in opposite directions – like I'm being torn apart. Even admitting that I feel jealous of Nicole is a challenge. Instead of admitting that I feel jealous I've accused Michael of not being fair enough, or I become suspicious of Nicole, thinking that she's plotting to take Michael away from me behind my back.

I realize that it's time for me to step completely into adulthood and to put on my big girl pants, otherwise I fear that I'll make myself sick again by carrying this anxiety around. I have to figure out a way to communicate what I'm feeling without making a mess of things by becoming defensive or by not be honest about how I really feel. I offer a silent prayer and I ask for Allah to help me.

Chapter Five

Change

A baby.

My mind has completely gone blank except for those two words: A BABY. It echoes across my psyche like a skip in a record: A BABY. A BABY. A BABY.

Gabriel has fallen asleep in his car seat in the back, and Michael and I remain in our seats up front, parked in his car in our driveway. The incessant creak of crickets fills the silence around us and the rectangular Tupperware container holding Nicole's lasagna and sweet potato pie rests warmly in my lap as my mind spins dizzily. I lean my head against the headrest and turn my head to gaze out the window at the clear black sky, searching for the moon but only finding darkness.

Michael knows me well enough to quietly allow me to process what he has just told me, and he doesn't make a sound as he holds my hand loosely in his. I wait for tears to form but there aren't any. No tears. No anger. No objections. Just a still, catatonic resignation. After all, I knew this was coming. I just didn't think it would arrive so soon.

Suddenly my recent dreams make more sense to me, and I wonder how far along Nicole is in the pregnancy. The sadness that I feel about the dwindling of our friendship turns into defeat as the fact that it is Michael sitting here telling me this information and not Nicole hits home. I can clearly remember the day when I told her about my being pregnant with Gabriel and the shared excitement and joy between us, or so I had thought, but I'm hearing this news from Michael and somehow it feels like a betrayal more than a joy. Had she been hiding this from me? And if she has – why? My dreams seem to have been telling me that she had.

Is this the end of our friendship? Are we destined to just be co-wives who hold each other at arm's length and to simply treat each other with cordial, good manners without the depth of the spiritual and mental friendship that we once had? I'm too shocked from this news to form a meaningful statement so I stick to the deen, and to what I've learned in Islam.

I sit up and face my husband, doing my best to smile, and I say, "Congratulations, hon. May Allah Ta'aala bless you both, and the baby."

Michael's eyes softly probe mine and he tries to smile back, but we're mirroring each other's expressions. I see the same faithful, and dutiful conviction in his features that I'm feeling in my heart. I know now that he has been keeping this from me and I wonder for a moment if he is hiding his happiness because he's afraid that I might be hurt by it.

"May Allah Ta'aala bless *us all,* this is *our* family," he responds, and squeezes my hand affectionately. "This is a blessing for all of us. Our family is growing."

I nod my head with more exuberance than I'm feeling, and I smile wider, keeping my emotional mask in place, but my cheeks are starting to hurt, and my face feels tight from the act. I'm more than ready to get out of this car and to retreat to my bedroom where I can sort this out.

I want to ask him why Nicole isn't sharing this information with me or why we aren't having this conversation together as a family, but I don't. Although he and I haven't spoken aloud to each other about the status of our family it is obvious to us both that we are struggling to maintain the family ties. Michael has been working late too for the past few weeks, so he and I hardly get to spend time together either. When we are together, we tend to bicker over little things or to retreat emotionally to avoid arguing. The vision of our family unit seems to be getting blurrier and blurrier to me as the weeks progress. Maybe this baby will bring us back into focus.

"Al Hamdulilah," I say and I lean over to kiss his cheek before reaching for the door handle. "Can you bring Gabey inside for me before you head over to Nicole's? My hands are full."

I lift the Tupperware container and my purse in his direction, although he obviously sees that my hands are full, but I don't know what else to say or do.

"Yeah. Of course," he hurries to reply, relieved that the announcement is over and done with.

He climbs out of the car and walks around to the passenger side to get Gabriel from the car seat while I open the front door and put my purse and the Tupperware container on the table in the narrow hallway beside the shoe shelf and coat rack. I take off my jacket and hang it up, and slip off my shoes, before returning to the open doorway just as Michael reaches it. Gabriel is sleeping soundly in Michael's arms and Michael hands him to me carefully, so we don't wake him up.

"The food for Nicole is right there on the table," I say quietly, gesturing with my head in the direction of the table. "And can you lock the door for me? I'm going to go ahead and bring him up."

Michael switches sleeping arrangements from week to week between the duplexes, and his week at Nicole's house starts tonight.

"Yes, of course," Michael says and gently holds my elbow before I can turn to go up the stairs.

I look up at him questioningly. He touches my cheek and kisses me softly. He meets my gaze before releasing my elbow.

"I love you, babe. This is good news. Get some rest. I'll call you tomorrow," he says, and that's all I need from him in this moment. His love and commitment is enough for me tonight.

"Ok. I love you too. As salaamu alaikum," I reply, feeling more at peace and less confused by that simple act of affection.

"Walaikum as salaam," he responds and waits at the foot of the stairs while I start the climb up with Gabey in my arms.

When I reach the second-floor landing, I hear the door close, and the lock turn over as Michael leaves. I walk into Gabey's bedroom and I lay him down in his crib to gingerly remove his shoes and jacket before going over to his dresser to get his pajamas. I return to the crib to remove his clothes and to check his Pull-Up to see if it's dry. I smile when I see that it is. My big boy is pretty much potty trained and able to go to the bathroom on his own now.

Tears prick at the back of my eyes at the realization of how he's growing and learning new things. Progressing. Things are changing and it suddenly seems a little too fast to me. I fight back tears as I put Gabriel into his pajamas.

I've been so emotional lately that I had placed a call to Dr. Alonzo's office on Friday and the nurse, Katie, had said that this is normal. She said that as my body rebuilds after the chemotherapy I'm going to go through changes in my hormones and biochemistry that will make me feel emotional, but not to worry. She said I need to exercise, and that I should start a personal exercise regimen to help with that. I make a mental note to get started tomorrow as I wipe away the tears.

Once I've finished dressing him he rolls over in the crib without waking, as if his body is instinctively more comfortable now. I cover him up with his blanket, turn the night light on, and leave his bedroom through the adjoining bathroom to enter mine.

I turn on the lamp on the bedside table in my room and I plop down onto the bed, laying flat on my back, to stare up at the ceiling with my hands folded across my heart. I try to imagine what life is going to be like now. A baby is going to affect us in more ways than one. Financially. Logistically. Emotionally. Spiritually. I know this. I've expected this. But the reality of it feels daunting. Especially when Nicole and I haven't had a decent conversation in weeks – almost two months now.

I begin to wonder if I've made the right decision when it comes to this lifestyle. I love everything about Islam, even polygyny and the potential that it embodies. I think about the Qur'anic verse that says that Allah never gives us more than we can bear, and I question whether I am strong enough to bear this. It takes an enormous amount of faith and fortitude to share a husband, and will I be able to continue this way when a baby is involved?

The cancer diagnosis has made me much more conscious of my mortality so I'm deeply aware of the fact that none of us here on this earth are promised tomorrow. We may come up with a detailed plan about how our lives will play out, but that doesn't mean that our lives will actually end up the way that we envision. I never imagined that I would have a life-threatening disease or be faced with having to share my husband, but I had. I had been prepared to leave this world if that was what was required of me, but it hadn't been. And now I find myself re-evaluating all of the decisions that I've made thus far in my life.

Do I really want to spend the rest of my life sharing my husband and living this way? Josh's face flits across my mind's eye at that question and I immediately feel uncomfortable. The fact that my subconscious has thrown his face up onto the screen of my mind is major. It had been nice talking to him, and even nicer discovering that he knew about Islam – that he had even considered converting to Islam himself. But more than that, talking with him made me feel seen. His attention made me feel less insecure. I recognize that there are many pathways available to me in this life and my question now is: am I on the right one?

I don't know the answer to that question at the moment, so I break down what I do know. I know that Islam has changed my life for the better. I know that Islam has changed me for the better, and that it has helped me to get through the pain and uncertainty of cancer and chemotherapy. I know that I'm a better person since being married to Michael, and I know that sharing a husband with Nicole has helped me to develop a closer relationship with Allah. I have come to feel a deep connection to Allah, to God, the Creator, Cherisher and Sustainer of all that exists, and this is a priceless gift that I will never turn away from. I will gladly spend the rest of my life practicing Islam. That much I do know.

In polygyny, I may have lost the exclusivity of a husband, but I've gained a closer relationship with Allah, and isn't that really what matters most in life?

I think about this, and I consider the changes to come. Michael and I will most likely have even less time to spend together than we already do, and all three of us are probably going to be busier and more stressed out as we face the increased expenses and responsibilities of two growing children to take care of, but what is faith if not the hope for things not seen? Its possible that we can handle this change without it becoming too much to bear . . .

I lean upon my faith, and I cling to the hope that Allah will provide for us from His abundance, and that Allah will allow us to draw even closer to Him, no matter the tests or trials that may come. With that in mind, I push myself up from my bed and decide that I need to make wudu and to make salaat. I need to pray. Whenever I'm confused or uncertain about something, more often than not, it is dua and salaat that clears my head and focuses my mind on that which is most important. I need that now more than ever.

Chapter Six

The Green-Eyed Monster

I watch Lisa with her new boyfriend, and I can't
stop the wave of envy that washes over me. We're
sitting on the bleachers in the gymnasium of
Nathaniel Greene Elementary school and he, I think
she said his name is Colby, is completely captivated
by her every move and word. And she is glowing –
absolutely radiant under his attention. She's
describing something that happened to her at work
earlier in the week and he's completely leaned in
and listening to her as if she's the most brilliant
person in the world. I smile, happy for her, and I try
to remember the last time that Michael looked at me
that way . . . college maybe . . . ? I shake off the
thought and the feelings provoked by it, and I
mentally lock up the green-eyed monster of
jealousy that has reared its head in the basement of
my mind.

The green-eyed monster appeared in my thoughts
and emotions the morning after Michael told me the
news about the baby last week and I haven't been
able to shake her since. She pops up whenever I
start to feel insecure about my relationship with

Michael. Mostly she just whispers snide remarks within my subconscious, but she's been popping up more frequently since Thursday when I caught a glimpse of Nicole and Michael through my living room window. Michael was rubbing the small round baby bump of Nicole's stomach and smiling, but I couldn't make out what they were saying. The green-eyed monster had quietly whispered, *Oooh, girl! You know that's not right! They should keep that to the confines of their house, not being all lovey-dovey right in front of you when they know you can see them!*

I had closed the curtains and gone back to reading my book, but I was scarred by seeing them that way. In this instance, she's shouting from behind the closed basement door of my mind: *that's a shame! College? That was years ago! Michael should be looking at you like that all the time, girl!*

I take a deep breath and look around the gym, keeping focused on the task at hand and trying to ignore the she-monster dwelling in my subconscious. It's a Saturday in late August and we're at the back-to-school event that Joshua's non-profit is hosting. I have the small digital camera from my office in my hand for taking photos for the quarterly newsletter and although it's the weekend, I can't help but feel like I'm working. Not all of "my people," as Joshua had referred to them had been able to make it. My two other best friends, Ellie and Amelia, couldn't come today, but Lisa had, and my little sister Jasmine is sitting on my opposite side, holding Gabriel in her arms. Our parents had other plans too, but our brother James is supposed to meet us here for the basketball tournament with our cousin Philip later. Aaron, who I don't technically consider one of "my people" is also here and mingling with some of the community organizers.

It's raining today so the back-to-school activities had been moved to the middle school instead of being held outside at the park. Families and teenagers from the East Side and surrounding neighborhoods have turned out in droves to support the event, and to take advantage of the freebies. There's music playing from a live local DJ set up on the far side of the gym and I see a camera man and journalist from the Providence Journal walking around within the crowds. Days like this make me love my job.

I snap some pictures as people start filing into the gymnasium and I spot some of the neighborhood kids rummaging through the free backpacks filled with free school supplies. They're already making trades and swapping out pens and notebooks with each other. Even Jasmine has taken a free backpack. Gabriel is still too small to appreciate the school supplies but he's clutching onto the lollipop that Jasmine bought for him from a candy booth and drooling stickily all over his little fist as he enjoys it. I snap a quick picture of him too, mostly because he just looks so cute and happy.

I hear basketballs being bounced along the gymnasium floor and I turn towards the sound to get a picture but there's a tall figure in front of me and the wide expanse of a man's chest covered by a black and white jersey that says COACH across the front. I look up to see Joshua's smiling face.

"Hey!" I say in surprise, more pleased than I should be by his appearance.

The green-eyed monster is banging on the basement door of my mind wanting to get out.

"Whatsup!" Joshua says back, his grin widening. "I'm glad you made it. I was hoping that the rain wouldn't make you have to stay away."

"Of course not! And I love the rain so that would never happen," I say with a smile, and I flinch inwardly. Was I just flirting?

My conscious mind goes into denial, insisting that I'm just being friendly, but the muffled voice of the she-monster in the basement shouts, *oh, yes you were, girl!*

"Who's this?" my sister Jasmine asks in her uncanny, old-soul tendency to catch a vibe even if she's not fully aware of what it is or what it means.

She eyes Joshua suspiciously. *She's team Michael all the way, isn't she*, the green-eyed monster remarks snidely.

"Is this Jasmine?" Josh asks incredulously before nudging my sister playfully on the shoulder. "You don't remember me? I went to high school with your sister. You're practically the same age she was back then! You guys came to watch some of my basketball games."

Jasmine doesn't look convinced, but she smiles cordially and replies, "Sorry. I don't remember."

"That's ok. Well, I'm glad you guys came out. What's up, Lisa-li. Hey, Colby! What's up, man?"

Joshua greets Lisa, and Colby, who he obviously knows pretty well by the short conversation that the two of them have about somebody named Kevin, and then Joshua looks back over at me, then at Gabey.

"And who's this handsome little man?" he says, reaching out a hand and leaning over to smile at Gabriel. "What's up little guy."

Gabriel manages to smile without taking the lollipop out of his mouth and allows Joshua to shake his clean hand.

"This is my son, Gabriel," I say, reaching into the diaper bag that I bring everywhere when Gabey's with me for a baby wipe to clean his face up a little.

"Wow! He's a handsome little guy. How old is he?" Joshua asks.

"Almost three," I respond as Jasmine takes over with another baby wipe to clean his fingers.

"I wouldn't believe it if I hadn't seen it with my own eyes. I can't believe you have a three-year old son," Joshua says.

He looks down at the camera in my hand and asks, "You're taking pictures?"

"Yes," I reply and lift it up. "For my job. We'll feature them in the newsletter at the end of the semester."

"Can I get copies? I didn't even think about doing that," he says.

"Of course. I'll email them to you next week," I say.

"Ok. Great. I was hoping to have an excuse to come by and pick them up, but everything is digital nowadays, so I'll have to think of another excuse to stop by your office," he says with a grin.

Jasmine stiffens instinctively beside me and eyes him again, and Lisa shoots me a I-told-you-there's-something-going-on-there look.

I don't know what to say in response to that, so I shift the conversation.

"Let me get a picture of you for the newsletter, coach," I say and I lift the camera towards him.

He smiles and strikes a pose. I seek refuge in Allah silently and instinctively to myself as I swoon a little bit internally. He's even more handsome now than he was in high school, and I sense remnants of adolescent infatuation lingering in my subconscious. This is *so* not good.

Yes, girl! You better seek refuge! Give him over here! I'll take care of that for you, the green-eyed monster shouts from the basement of my mind.

A referee blows a whistle, filling the gymnasium with the shrillness of it, and rescues me from an extremely uncomfortable situation. I feel heat rise up my neck and I don't even risk looking over at Lisa – she knows me too well and I know that she's got something to say.

"That's my cue. I've got to go. Nice seeing you," Josh says but he doesn't make a move to leave or to take his eyes from mine until I respond.

"Yes. You too," I say, embarrassed and feeling like an exposed nerve.

"See you, Colby. Later Lisa. It was nice seeing you again, Jasmine, and nice meeting you little man," he says in parting before bounding down the bleachers two at a time to join the basketball team of teens and pre-teens assembled on the gym floor.

"Later," Lisa responds slyly as he leaves, and she leans closer to me to murmur. "Oh. You're not going anywhere after this game. We need to talk."

Jasmine is staring straight ahead as if completely engrossed by what's going on below us on the court, but I can feel her radar bleeping and seeking out anything that she can possibly overhear from me or Lisa.

"Fine," I agree curtly and quietly, and with complete denial. "But there's nothing to talk about. I already told you about how he came by the Center for the interview with Shayleene."

Ooooooh. You better stop lying to your girl. You know you're feelin' that man, the she-monster comments.

I gaze forward at the basketball court and position the digital camera in front of my face under the pretense of taking more pictures to hide my emotions.

Be quiet, you, I tell the she-monster firmly.

She chuckles wickedly.

Chapter Seven

Heartbreak

"Wow. Well. We knew this was coming. How are you feeling?" my mother asks with concern evident on every inch of her face.

I've just told her the news about the baby. It has taken me two weeks to tell her and she's the first person I've revealed this to. Her main worry lately is my health and I know that her mind went immediately to how the news about the baby might affect my stress levels. She's sitting beside me at the table in the conference room at the Center and watches me carefully as she chews a mouthful of chicken curry.

"I feel good," I respond after swallowing a mouthful of lamb saag. "My health has actually been getting increasingly better since I started back to work and even the doctor at the Dana Farber Institute was surprised at how well I've been doing. He said that he doesn't see a need for radiation treatment at this point and he scheduled an appointment for a follow up in December."

And it's true. I do feel good overall. My hair is growing back steadily, I'm a whopping 127 lbs, and since I've been exercising, I've been able to gain a semblance of control over my emotions. I still feel a little insecure about my marriage, and the green-eyed monster in my mind continues to stalk me, but I'm not about to tell my mother that, not now when she is finally starting to worry less about my health. Being back at work has been great and I feel even more relieved to be able to contribute financially to the family again which has been a huge uplift. Nicole and I still haven't been talking much, but I've given that issue over to God and I've been prayerfully and patiently waiting for a breakthrough.

"That's great, baby!" my mother exclaims, and her eyes brighten. "Make sure you don't let the idea of a new baby stress you out, though. I know how you hold everything in, so you had better talk to me if this becomes an issue for you."

"I will, ma. Promise," I say, and I lean over to kiss her cheek.

She smiles and asks, "So how far along is she?"

I swallow a drink of iced tea and answer, "Three months. She's due in March."

My mother nods thoughtfully and I can see the gears of her mind churning as she does the mental math to calculate when conception had likely occurred. I shake my head and hide behind my straw as I take another swallow of iced tea. I hope she doesn't ask me about it. That's been one of my issues and I know it will trigger the green-eyed monster. From my own calculations, it had to have happened sometime in June, soon after she moved from Boston to RI.

That was three months ago. Its September now and my hopes for improving our relationships are feeling out of reach these days. The three of us don't spend any time together anymore and our relationships have divided into partnerships with Nicole and Michael on one side and me and Michael on the other. It's been weird and awkward, and as a result, I feel like a stranger in our family dynamic. Michael and I are arguing frequently lately and although I'm trying not to let that get to me, it's starting to.

The building alarm chimes to announce that someone has entered through the front door and my mother and I both turn our heads towards the entrance of the conference room expectantly. Michael steps into view holding two large paper bags filled with take out.

"Looks like we had the same idea today, mom," he says and carries the food into the conference room.

"Hey there son-in-law!" my mother says and smiles brightly in welcome before standing up to hug him.

He puts the bags down and hugs my mother warmly, dwarfing her small form with his. He then turns to me and hugs me too.

"Hmm. You guys got Indian. I brought Chinese. I should have called first, but I wanted to surprise you," he says and laughs.

"I'm so glad you did," I say, excited to see him, especially after the bleak thoughts I'd just been having.

My mother starts packing up her aluminum to-go container of chicken curry, naan bread, and basmati rice.

"I'm going to get on out of here and let the two of you have some time together," my mother says happily but she discreetly doesn't mention that I've just told her about the baby.

"No, mom. You were here first, I should have called," Michael objects.

My mother shakes her head authoritatively as she shrugs into her sweater and grabs her purse from the back of the chair that she was sitting in.

"Mm-mm. I insist. I see her all the time around here," she says and hugs me tightly.

She hugs Michael and waves at the both of us before exiting the conference room and heading for the front door. Michael sits down in the chair that my mother has vacated as I sit back down in mine.

"This is a nice surprise," I say sincerely. "What has you over here on this side of town?"

"Nicole's doctor's appointment was today, over on Waterman Street," he says and takes a forkful of my half-eaten lamb saag.

My body tenses reflexively at his announcement.

"Oh, that's right, I forgot," I say as I remember him telling me that this morning when he came to pick up Gabey for driving him to daycare.

Michael starts unpacking the Chinese food that he's brought. I get a whiff of General Tso Chicken, our family favorite, as he empties the first paper bag.

"Where is she?" I ask, trying to sound nonchalant and wondering if she's waiting in his car outside.

"She had to go back to work. I met her at the doctor's office, so she had her car and I had mine," he says and opens the paper carton of vegetable fried rice. "You want some?"

I nod yes and push my container of lamb saag and basmati rice towards him for a few scoops of rice.

"You look pretty today," he says with a smile as he adds a spoonful of General Tso Chicken on top of the fried rice.

Heat rises up my neck and into my cheeks under his gaze and I smile back, embarrassed by the compliment. He hasn't said anything like that to me in a really long time and I don't realize that I have some belligerent feelings about that until this moment. Thoughts from the argument that we'd had the night before prevent me from enjoying the compliment for longer than two seconds.

"I, uh, thank you," I reply, and if I can hear the lack of conviction in my voice then I know he can too.

His smile slowly fades, and he leans back into his chair, becoming thoughtful. He continues to gaze at me, his eyes probing into mine, but he doesn't ask me anything. I lower my gaze and lean back into my chair as well, pushing lamb and chicken around in the aluminum container and waiting for him to say something first.

I know that's right, girl, the green-eyed monster instigates. *He better speak up and act like he cares! After his comments last night, the ball is in his court!*

I shush her internally and lock her back in the basement of my mind, but I cannot ignore the feelings that are bubbling up to the surface of my heart. A widening distance has formed between Michael and I despite my efforts to keep that from happening. The basketball tournament and my reaction to Joshua's attention had been an eye-opener for me so I had tried to talk to Michael about some of my insecurities last night, hoping for reassurance from him, but he had shut me down. I know that lunch today is his peace offering for some of the things that were said but it's hard to let my guard down.

His points were completely valid and helpful for steering me in the right direction in terms of the deen. and how I should feel about myself and about our relationship as a Muslim woman, but I didn't want to be steered – I wanted to be heard. He couldn't seem to switch gears from treating me like a child to treating me as a wife since the cancer diagnosis no matter how much I tried to express how I feel, and last night had been no different from many nights that we've spent together lately. He had reminded me to read the hadeeth and to consider looking up verses from the Qur'an for guidance concerning my feelings. Ultimately the conversation had ended with me in tears and with him walking away. I'm not about to put myself in that situation again, no matter how happy I am about this surprise visit, so I continue eating my lunch.

He eventually gets the hint that I'm giving him the silent treatment because he pulls out a paper plate and some plastic utensils and condiments from the second paper bag and begins piling food onto it. We eat in silence. I don't look up again from my food until all of it is gone. When I look at him there's a slight frown around his eyebrows as he continues to eat and as much as I want to ease his frustration, I refuse to say anything. The last thing I want is to initiate a conversation that will have me become an emotional, crying mess here at work.

It's hard to believe that there was a time when Michael and I would talk for hours because we never wanted to be apart from one another. I remember the days when we were together every day and every night for almost a year, and we never got bored or argued or were at a loss for something to say. But now, sitting here in silence, I feel heartbreak. It's like we don't know each other anymore.

The front door alarm chimes again and I hear Shayleene and Carol's voices as they return from their lunch break. It sounds like they've stopped in front of Carol's office next door to finish a conversation they had been having.

"I guess I'll head out," Michael says quietly to me as he finishes the final forkful of his lunch.

"Ok," I reply, making an extra effort to put as much affection into my tone as possible.

I hope that he understands that I'm not saying anything for the sake of self-preservation, and I make a mental note to be sure to say that to him later, but for the first time in our relationship, I'm not sure if he understands me at all. It breaks my heart that his surprise visit has ended up this way and I fervently blink back the tears that are forming. I don't want it to end this way, but I also don't want to pour my heart out to him again and be treated like my feelings are insignificant. We clean up the table side by side, in silence.

Chapter Eight

Searching for Meaning

I take the curve around the outdoor track at Rhode Island College, jogging a little too fast, and I trip over my own foot, distracted by my thoughts. I maintain my balance, miraculously avoiding a tumble onto the asphalt, and I slow my pace. Running has always helped to clear my head and I need it today more than I have in a long time. I can't get the previous night's argument between Michael and I out of my head.

It's chilly for mid-October and the weather forecast has predicted a light snowfall tonight. I can see my breath in front of me as I run, and my chest is beginning to burn from inhaling the cold air. Deciding that this will be my last lap, I slow my pace further so my body can start to cool down.

The argument keeps spontaneously replaying itself in my head and I can't stop thinking about what was said. We never used to argue this way and I hate it. The worst part about it is that once you say a thing, you can't un-say it, and the hurt tends to linger. I think about the many conversations that he and I have had about polygyny, and about his reasons for choosing another wife, but I cannot find any meaning from any of them, at least nothing that makes me feel like I've made a good decision by agreeing to it.

He has said that his decision doesn't have anything to do with his love for me and that it doesn't change, decrease or devalue his love or commitment to our marriage, but I'm unsure of how to interpret that. He has even said that it was a completely spiritual decision and an act of worship to God, but I'm beginning to feel a strain upon my psyche because although his reasons for entering polygyny are clear to him, my reasons for entering haven't been completely clear to me.

I had initially agreed to polygyny because I had prayed about it, and because I had thought it was the right decision to make as a sincere believer in Islam, but the more I've learned about the religion the harder it is to lean upon that reasoning for comfort when I feel jealous or not loved enough. I've been reading through translations of the hadeeth recently and the more I learn about the sunnah of the Prophet Muhammad the more I realize how confused I've been about the world and my place in it.

As a small-town girl from a predominantly Christian community and family environment where everyone pretty much knows each other, my life has been sheltered and restricted to a small slice of reality. Learning about Islam and its rich history, and about the vastness of the different Muslim experiences around the world has truly been mind-opening, and as a result, polygyny has begun to feel like wearing shoes that are too tight. Like I've made a premature decision.

I've come to understand that polygyny was prescribed during a time of warfare when there was a surplus of widows and orphans in the Muslim community, and at that time, most women weren't able to make their own living in the world, so marriage was a mercy that was of great benefit at that specific time in history, but it is not a required practice according to Islam. In my haste to be a good Muslim woman, did I choose a way of life that I don't really want – something that is not required of me? I had thought that Michael was my soulmate, but is he really? What is a soul mate and is it possible for him to be both my and Nicole's soulmate?

Uh, I don't think so, the green-eyed monster states firmly.

I ignore her, but the essence of the argument last night was about this very issue, and I wonder if I've made the right choices concerning my own life. I used to think that Michael was my soul mate, and last night I tried to tell him this and how hard it is to accept that he loves me as much as I love him when he has taken another wife, but he was dismissive about it. His argument was that the concept of a soul mate is a Western idea that isn't based in the scripture and although I could understand that, it hurt that he didn't reassure me of his love but rather chose to argue semantics and cultural history with me. We went back and forth for an hour, as quietly as possible so we wouldn't wake up Gabey, but in the end, I was in tears in the bedroom, and he was downstairs in the living room. I woke up early to go for a run and left a note on the living room table letting him know and asking him to listen out for Gabey while he slept on the couch.

This morning I feel scarred and weary from last night's mental boxing match. I focus on trying to figure out what I want and what I expect from our marriage. He may be right about the concept of a soul mate being of a philosophy outside of the fold of Islam, but love and equity between spouses certainly isn't. I need to know that he loves me at least just as much as I love him, and lately I'm not feeling like he does. I've survived the cancer that had ravaged my body and now I want to live each moment of my life to the fullest. I want to experience all that I have a right to experience. I want to be happy again. I don't want to waste one minute or to live without the fullness of all that Islam promises, especially when it comes to marriage.

I finish the lap and walk over to the grass to stretch. The sky is overcast and there's a cool breeze in the air rustling through the dry brown and orange leaves that have fallen from the surrounding trees. The breeze makes me shiver when it blows against the sweat on my neck despite how hot my body feels.

Something that Michael said to me in the heat of the argument that we had last night flashes across my mind suddenly. *"You haven't been yourself for weeks and I'm tired of walking on eggshells around you!"*

And he was right, I haven't been, but in my mind, I think I'm entitled to feel a little not-like-myself after three months of chemotherapy treatment that had killed off millions of my brain and body cells. I'd asked my primary care doctor about how I've been feeling lately, even though I've been exercising, and she said that I'm likely experiencing what they call chemo brain. She had explained that cancer patients sometimes experience cognitive impairment and/or dysfunction during or after treatment and it had been as if a lightbulb had turned on inside of my head. I haven't been "myself" for weeks because "myself" literally has changed on a cellular level.

Anger washes over me as I remember his words and my mind instinctively searches for a clever retort, but I seek refuge in Allah, and I try to clear my thoughts and seek a state of peace instead. Focusing on my muscles, I reach towards my foot, stretching sideways over my leg, and I take a deep, calming breath.

"Jo! Hey! What are you doing here?" I hear a male voice call out to me and it takes me a few seconds to recognize that it's my brother James.

I look up to see him walking towards me, and then I'm shocked to my bones to see Joshua walking beside him. This can't be happening to me.

Oh, it is girl. You can't seem to get away from this here lesson, the green-eyed monster says.

I smile stiffly at the two of them, hoping that the smile looks real, and I put on my emotional mask. The green-eyed monster won't go into the basement of my mind this time, so I'm forced to face this situation with her nagging voice hovering around in my head.

"Hey!" I say back and I sit up straight. "I just finishing running."

James and Joshua drop to the dry grass in front of me and make themselves comfortable, like they're not in any rush to get anywhere.

"What are you doing here?" I ask, masking my discomfort.

"Uh, I go to school here, remember?" James replies with a grin. "This is my space. And your boy here is a coach for the basketball team so you're the one trespassing."

He laughs and I force a laugh out too, lowering my head so he can't tell that the laughter hasn't reached my eyes.

Yup, that's my boy! Showing up at just the right place and just the right time, the green-eyed monster agrees.

"Right. My bad," I say, hoping I don't sound tense or look mental, so I try to joke. "Forgive me for trespassing."

James laughs again and asks, "Where's Mike? I thought you two worked out together on the weekends?"

"He had to work. He got a new investor for the business so they're at the office working through some of the paperwork," I reply, and I say astagfirullah internally, seeking Allah's forgiveness for lying, then changing the subject. "You have track practice today?"

"Yeah. In about 15 minutes. I'm early," James says but he finally realizes that something is wrong with me, and his expression sobers. "What's going on? You ok?"

I lower my gaze as tears prick my eyes. I don't know what it is about me that makes me cry when someone asks if I'm ok when I'm not ok but it's irritating. He's another one who knows me too well for me to easily hide behind my emotional mask.

"I'm fine," I say but my voice cracks and I know that he has noticed the suppressed tears. "Nothing's going on. I'm actually finished, and I was just getting ready to go home."

I stand up and pretend to brush grass from my sweatpants until I've completely blinked away the tears and my eyes are dry. Track team members begin to trickle onto the field, and I notice the track coach crossing the grass from the opposite side. James and Joshua stand up after me as I try to avoid James' gaze.

"Here comes your coach and the team," I say, and I pull my car keys from my sweatpants pocket.

I hug him tightly and give him a quick kiss on the
cheek.

"I gotta go. I'll see you tomorrow at mom and dad's
for dinner," I say to him and I give a quick wave of
good-bye to Joshua before turning to hurry to my
car in the nearby parking lot.

"All right," James calls out uncertainly from behind
me. "But I'm coming by your house after practice to
check on you so have food. I love you! As Salaamu
Alaikum!"

Now that I'm far enough away I turn back around
and shout, "Ok! Love you too! Walaikum as
salaam!"

And turning around was a good idea because I now
see that Joshua is following me. He waves to get my
attention and to gesture for me to wait for him. I
don't want to, but I don't want to be rude to him
either. I wait for him, and he reaches me quickly.

"Can I walk you to your car?" he asks with an
expression of concern on his face.

The tears return and I look away to compose
myself. He gently grabs my elbow and begins
walking with me towards the parking lot. We walk
in silence, side-by-side, and his presence is
comforting. By the time we reach the parking lot I

have blinked the tears away and I've gotten myself together enough to speak.

"Thank you. My car is right here. I always park close to the fence," I say, but my voice sounds throaty with emotions as my mask begins to crack.

"That's smart. And the safest place to park," he says encouragingly.

I look up at him and see the same expression of concern on his face as when he asked to walk me to my car. It almost makes me cry but I use every ounce of strength that I have to hold the tears back.

"Thanks again," I say, and I manage a small grateful smile as I reach for the door handle.

"No problem," he says and it seems like he doesn't want me to go.

I unlock the car door and get in while he stands close by. It looks like he's trying to think of how best to say something so I give him a few seconds, but I know that my mask won't last for much longer.

"Listen. I don't want to pry, but you don't seem ok. People talk. I don't know your man, but I've heard a few things. You've got my number. You can call me anytime," he says compassionately.

I open my mouth to object, and he steps closer to the car door and gently interjects before I can say anything.

"I know all about the rules of Islam, I'm not trying to disrespect you or him. I just want you to know that it matters to me if you're upset about something and I can be a friendly ear," he says earnestly.

I believe him, and I'm touched, but I wonder about what he's heard and who he has heard it from. Instead of opening that can of worms, I nod my head and thank him again.

"I appreciate that," I reply as calmly as I can. "I have to go but thank you. Take care."

"You take care too. As salaamu Alaikum," he says to me.

"Walaikum as salaam," I respond, and I wave at him before closing the car door and starting the engine.

My mask crumbles when I reach Smith Street and the tears that I've been holding back stream down my face. I don't bother to wipe them as the emotional dam that I've built breaks. The short drive home is a thoughtful drive as I consider the path in front of me. My heart is pounding in my chest and my hands are shaking when I pull up to our duplex.

Why would "people" be talking about Michael or anything that has to do with Michael and me? And what would they be saying. I decide that I don't want to know. Regardless of what anyone may or may not be saying, I realize that I have a choice to make. I'm either in this marriage all the way, or I'm not. And I don't know what to choose.

Chapter Nine

Meltdown

"How is that fair?!" I shout at Michael, unable to keep myself from lashing out. "We were married first!"

That's right, girl! You tell him! Who does he think he is? Don't you let him get away with that, the green-eyed monster instigates yet again, but this time we are completely in sync with one another.

"What do you mean?!" Michael shouts back. "How can you even ask me something like that?! It's fair because I have a duty to her just like I have one to you. I'm not about to get a divorce from Nicole just because you've changed your mind about wanting to live polygyny."

I'm in tears, my head is spinning, and I feel like I'm about to start hyperventilating. Nothing makes sense in this moment and all I can think to myself is: this man is my enemy. It's the middle of the night but I can't stay here for another moment. I have to get out of here.

I jump out of the bed and I go over to the dresser to get a pair of pants and a sweatshirt. I pull the jeans up under my nightgown and pull the sweatshirt over it hurriedly, afraid that he's going to try to question me or stop me.

He's only wearing his undershirt and boxer shorts, and even in my manic state I realize that I have the advantage if I hurry.

"Joanna. What are you doing?" he asks with exasperation.

We've been arguing for the past thirty minutes. I don't reply and instead I go through the top drawer for a pair of socks. I put the socks on and then go over to the closet for my sneakers.

He gets out of the bed and follows me to the closet.

"Jo. Stop. Where are you going?" Michael asks, more exasperated and obviously frustrated. "It's the middle of the night!"

He reaches for my shoulder, but I shake him off and push past him, rushing towards the stairs. Crying hysterically, I reach the bottom of the stairs and snatch my purse from the wall hook before leaving, slamming the front door closed behind me. A light snow is falling as I rush to the car and my hands are shaking as I rummage through my purse for the keys. I find them and unlock the door to climb inside and I slam the door closed frantically. Just then Michael opens the front door, having put on a pair of sweatpants, and he hurries towards the car in his bare feet as I start up the engine. I back out down the driveway and drive away as fast as I can.

Don't cry, girl. He's not worth your tears. You don't need him, the green-eyed monsters says.

Tears blur my vision as I drive, and I can't stop sobbing. I cry the whole way to my parents' house, ignoring the monster in the basement of my mind as best as I can but she makes sense to me in my current state. Why should I stay married if deep down I don't want to? All he does is work lately, and argue with me when we're together, and who knows what he might be doing when he's at Nicole's house. He's probably working so much during our week so he'll have more free time to spend with her when it's their week together.

You know he probably is, the green-eyed monster agrees.

I've calmed down a little as I turn onto my parents' street and by God's grace, I've made it safely to their house on the East Side. I let myself in with the key that I still have, and I walk quietly into the living room at the front of the house where I sit down on the couch to cry, careful not to get too loud. I feel like I'm losing my mind. Nothing makes sense and all I can think is that I want my mother.

I hear soft footsteps coming down the stairs and I look over to the right to see my mother's robed body coming towards me. For a second, I wonder if I'm hallucinating but as she gets closer and turns on the lamp on the side table by the couch, I know that she is real.

"Baby, what's the matter?" she asks, squinting sleepily at me and rubbing her eyes as she sits down beside me on the couch.

I throw my arms around her and bury my face on her chest.

"Shhhhh," she says soothingly and rubs my back gently as I cry. "Just tell me if everything is ok, Jo? Where's Gabey? Is someone hurt?"

I realize in shock that I've left without my baby, and I cry even harder, shaking my head and I manage to mumble, "No, nobody is hurt. He's with Michael. We had another argument. I just needed to go."

"Oh, baby," my mother says sympathetically and continues to rub my back. "It's ok, honey. It's' going to be ok."

"It's not going to be ok. I don't want this, mom. I don't want to share my husband. I thought I could do it, but I can't. It hurts too much," I sob, and I sound intelligible to my own ears, but my mother seems to have understood.

"It's ok to change your mind, sweetheart, but are you sure about this? You've been so emotional lately, baby. What made you change your mind?" my mother asks gently.

The sobbing quiets down and eventually stops as I try think clearly and to figure out what has made me change my mind. Tears continue to stream down my face, and it feels like there's a hole in my chest, but no one reason stands out. It's everything. It's the fact that a baby is coming into the family. It's the fact that Nicole couldn't tell me herself that she was pregnant. It's because Michael has been spending so much time at work. It's imaging what he and Nicole are doing when he's at her house next door. It's surviving the cancer and now not knowing what to do with my life. It's the attention from Joshua and feeling like there's another path for me besides the one that I'm walking right now.

Car headlights flash across the living room windows, creating two small orbs of light against the curtains before the car parks in front of the house and the headlights go out when the engine is turned off. I instinctively know that it's Michael. The doorbell rings and my mother puts enough space between the two of us to look at my face. She knows it's him too.

"What do you want me to say? Should I let him in?" she asks me.

I sit up and wipe the tears from my face with the sleeve of my sweatshirt before I respond.

"I'll get it. You can go back to bed. I'll be ok," I say.

My throat aches from crying, my voice is hoarse when I speak and I can only imagine what my face must look like, but she concedes reluctantly.

"I'll be right upstairs, honey," she says and kisses my cheek before leaving the living room.

I get up from the couch and go to the front door and open it. Michael's frantic expression dissolves and is replaced with relief when he sees me. More tears form and run down my face at the sight of him.

"I tried to call you, but you left your cell phone at the house," he says, handing it to me.

I take it and put it into the back pocket of my jeans then ask, "Where's Gabey?"

"With Nicole," Michael answers.

I wipe the tears from my face and stare expectantly at him. It's still snowing, and a thin layer of snow is covering the sidewalk and the bushes beside the front steps. A cool breeze dries the remaining wetness on my face, making my skin feel taut and stiff. I stand there, staring at him, unable to speak and waiting for him to say something. He finally does.

"Come home, Jo. I'm sorry for yelling. Let's talk this through, babe," he says to me, and his expression is pleading.

He reaches out his hand to me, but I refuse and lower my gaze to the porch. Rather than let anymore heat out of the house, I open the door wider and gesture for him to come in. I close the door behind him, and we walk over to the couch to sit.

"What is there left to talk about?" I ask him as tears threaten to form again but I resist them.

"Everything," he replies earnestly. "Have you even thought this through completely? How can you expect me to get a divorce from Nicole? Especially with the baby coming?"

In my mind the answer is simple, and I don't see any irrationality. Just like he married Nicole so easily, he can divorce her just as easily and we can go back to how things were before this whole thing ever happened. The green-eyed monster is unusually quiet in this moment and that puzzles me. Confusion must have been apparent on my face.

"Jo? Are you with me?" Michael asks and his expression looks concerned when I meet his gaze.

"You've been all over the place lately, babe. When was the last time you made prayer? Can we pray together, babe?" he asks me, and the tears return but this time I can't resist them.

Tears roll down my face and over my chin. His mentioning prayer opens a floodgate of emotions that I can't resist, and there's only one, aching question that fills my mind: oh Allah, why is this happening to me? I can't remember the last time that I made prayer today – was it maghrib? Am I losing my mind? And if polygyny is a good thing, why am I feeling so much pain and confusion?

I nod my head yes and I let Michael hug me. I want to ask him, these questions, but I don't. Instead, I ask them over and over again in my head, like a prayer, and I cry in his arms. He holds me for several long moments and waits until I've stopped crying before he lets me go.

Like a compass, he has pointed me in the right direction, and I remember how it feels to be loved by him. He no longer feels like my enemy, and I feel ashamed for having thought that. Michael is doing what he believes Allah wills for him, and who am I to ask him to change that? I hold on to him and I realize that only Allah can help me through this pain and confusion that I'm feeling, and that prayer is a necessary resource for attaining that help. All of the arguing and all of the harsh words from over the past few weeks have shaken me to my core, have scarred me, and him too, I think, but tonight it feels like we are finally turning a corner in the right direction.

Not once over the past month have we stopped to pray together in the face of an argument. We've instead stood against each other, each of us wanting to be right and neither of us wanting to be wrong. We've debated our points at one another, like two opponents, rather than listening to one another like two teammates. His eyes are wet with tears as he looks at me and brushes his hand across my cheek.

"Let's go home," he says. "We can get through this together."

I nod my head and stand up.

"I just need to tell my mother I'm ok. I'll be right back," I say and turn towards the stairs.

Tonight has broken us both, but I know that we can heal.

Chapter Ten

Temptation

"Come on, Jo. Enough is enough. Get your coat right now or I'll get it for you and drag you from this house," Lisa demands firmly.

She knows all about the meltdown I had a few weeks ago and she is determined to get me out of the house for a night of fun. I've been dragging my feet, trying to get out of going but she's not having it. I look myself over one more time, and I actually feel pretty in my burgundy abaya and matching khimar. There's gold embroidery along the rim of the belled sleeves and along the rim of the khimar and the gold bangle bracelets that I'm wearing add just the right amount of bling. My physical health is good, although my emotional state goes up and down, and I want to enjoy myself tonight, but I can't ignore the nagging guilt in the back of my mind.

Guilt because I know that Joshua is going to be there. Yes, I'll be in a room full of people so it's not like we will be alone together. Yes, Michael knows exactly where I am going, how long I'll be there, and when I'm coming home. And yes, it's a completely job-related event so it's not like I can even get out of it, but I still feel guilty.

I feel guilty because I've taken extra care doing my hair (even though it's covered by my khimar) and picking out my outfit. I feel guilty because I'm wearing lipstick when I usually never do for events like this, and I feel guilty because there's a flutter of anticipation in my chest at the thought of seeing Joshua again. The guilt has made me try to get out of going to the reception and lecture that the Center is hosting but Lisa is pumped about meeting the guest speaker for this year's ethnicity in America lecture, and we're each other's plus one since her boyfriend Colby has to work and Michael isn't going. I put on my shoes, and I grab my dressy winter coat from the closet.

I haven't told Lisa that Joshua might be going, but she knows about what happened the last time I saw him. I'm not even sure that he will be there, but he had emailed me earlier that day to confirm the start time for the lecture, so I assume that he is.

"Ok, ok, bossy lady. I'm ready," I reply, and I start walking towards my open bedroom door.

Michael has Gabey with him next door at Nicole's for the night, so the house is quiet and dark when we reach the bottom of the stairs. I had hoped that

Michael would be able to come with us tonight, but it's Nicole's week to spend time with him and I didn't want to ask him to switch the schedule around, mainly because we have gone a whole two weeks without arguing and I don't want to rock the boat.

Progress has been slow, but steady, since our last argument, so I feel even more guilty about tonight. The green-eyed monster is trying to persuade me to not feel guilty, but she's muffled by the dhikr to Allah that I'm making in my head. I still feel torn about sharing Michael with Nicole, but we've committed to moving forward patiently and prayerfully together. He and I have also agreed to be more open with each other and to listen better if an issue comes up, and so far, so good. Thus, the guilt.

I haven't seen Joshua since that Saturday at RIC and I've resisted the temptation to reach out to him via email about his cryptic statement concerning "people" talking, but I'm eager to see him again. It's not because I'm considering actually taking him up on the offer to call him, but because I like the attention. I offer an astagfirullah and decide that I will do my best to stay as far away from him as possible, if he even goes.

The green-eyed monster rears up at my internal conflict and mutters, *If you're going to be saying that all night, girl, you might as well just stay home.*

Lisa is waiting impatiently as I lock my front door. I'm trapped in a dilemma of my own making and there's no turning back now. I can't let Lisa down by not going tonight, and I'm determined to work on my marriage, despite the flattery from Joshua, so I take a deep breath and button my coat.

Winter has come early this year and it's snowing tonight as we leave my duplex and walk over to Lisa's car where it's parked along the sidewalk. We maneuver as quickly as we dare along the slick driveway and sidewalk in the high heels that we're wearing, and we eagerly climb into her car to get out of the cold.

"I must admit, I was hoping to see Nicole and to get a look at her baby bump," Lisa says as she starts the car's engine. "You guys still aren't talking?"

I flinch a little at the mention of Nicole and how things are between her and I and respond, "No, not really. Well, we talk about superficial stuff, but it feels forced and uncomfortable sometimes."

Lisa makes a sad face and reaches over to pat my arm and replies, "Don't worry. It will get better. And if it doesn't, remember your promise to me?"

We stop at a traffic light, and she makes eye contact with me to confirm that I remember. I do.

"Yes, ma'am," I respond and smile sadly. "I promised that if this becomes too much for me then I'll reconsider polygyny."

She nods firmly and turns her eyes back to the road.

"Ok. Good," she says.

She and I had had a long talk and a good cry when I'd told her about the argument that Michael and I had had. I told her about how Michael and I had prayed salaat together after and how I felt calmer, and more peaceful after that, and although she listened and empathized, she had re-affirmed her belief that I shouldn't stay in the marriage if it becomes too hard to be happy in it. We had agreed on that whole-heartedly. And I had explained that patience and forgiveness are major cornerstones in Islam and that even if I don't feel "happy" all the time, by being patient with situations and by being willing to forgive and to seek forgiveness, there's a greater chance for producing lasting happiness.

We also agreed that patience and forgiveness are important for building any kind of relationship, especially a marriage. We all make mistakes. Human beings are flawed. If we're not patient with one another and willing to forgive each other when we offend one another then chaos usually follows. And I've had enough of chaos.

Mmm-hmm. If that's true then why are you all dressed up tonight, the green-eyed monster taunts me.

I recite more dhikr of remembrance in my head to silence her.

"So, we're really going to be able to meet him, right?" Lisa asks me excitedly, interrupting my thoughts. "I have my copy of his book in my purse. I want to get his autograph."

I smile, thankful for the conversation, and respond, "We should. There shouldn't be more than 50 people at the reception so as long as we make our move early in the evening we should get the chance to meet him. People are incredibly chatty at these functions so we have to be forceful."

"Oh, I'm ready," Lisa states and grins, and then switches gears. "Why were you acting so weird earlier, like you don't want to go? Am I missing something?"

Go on, tell her, the green-eyed monster insists.

I've made all five of my prayers today, on time, and I've been offering dhikr all day, yet here she remains! I lock her in the basement of my mind and answer Lisa.

"Nothing. I wasn't acting weird. How was I weird?" I ask defensively, unable to admit my feelings concerning Joshua even to her.

"You were just so draggy and unwilling to get dressed. I practically had to pick your outfit for you. Is it because Michael isn't going?" she probes, her best-friend radar in full effect.

Nope. It's because Joshua is *going,* the monster says from the basement.

"Kind of," I answer.

"Well stop. We're still going to have a good time," she says. "I know you don't drink anymore but we'll still enjoy the night eating fancy food and drinking from fancy glasses."

"Yes. We're going to be fancy tonight," I say with the first genuine smile I've felt in weeks.

She grins back and says, "Of course we are! We're fancy ladies. Fancy smanshy ladies."

We both laugh at that and fall into the silly, carefree banter that makes our friendship so much fun.

"Fancy smanshy ladies going to a fancy smanshy reception to mingle with fancy smanshy people," I say, and we laugh some more.

We reach the university campus and struggle to find a parking spot. The snow has stopped falling but there's about an inch of it, soft and fluffy, covering the sidewalks so it's another ten minutes before we reach the venue across the main green. The small gathering hall is filled from wall to wall with students, faculty and guests eager to have a conversation with the speaker of tonight's event.

We check our coats at the entrance before walking into the reception area. Tables are set up throughout the room for people to stand at and drink or eat the hors d'oeuvres, but there are no chairs. Shayleene had insisted that there be no chairs because people would linger there instead of clearing the room and attending the lecture. The lecture is to be given in an hour in the adjoining lecture hall.

I spot Shayleene and Carol across the room beside the speaker, Dr. Cornell East, and Shayleene waves us over. Lisa squeezes my arm in anticipation as she sees him and does a little, discreet, happy dance, clicking her high heels against the hardwood floor. She pulls her book and a pen out of her purse as we walk over to them. Shayleene makes the introductions and Lisa wastes no time showing him her book and gushing over the content, all the while positioning the book in front of him for an autograph.

I think fleetingly about how obsessed we were with popular boy bands like New Edition and Troop when we were younger, and I compare how similar those feelings of obsession are to these feelings of obsession for Dr. Cornel East now that we're older. It's different now, of course, because we've actually read his books and his work has a greater impact on the progress of society, but the excitement is very similar. I wish I had been mindful enough to have brought my own copy of his book with me and I make a mental note to make sure that I buy another copy and stand in line for the book signing after the lecture.

We are only able to bask in his brilliance for about five minutes before we were elbowed out of the little circle around him by a pair of professors from the Africana Studies Department. Lisa nearly squeals with delight once we're out of hearing range.

"That was so dope," she says and grins at me.

"I agree," I say with a sigh as we walk over to the hors d'oeuvres station.

"I'm ready for some fancy smanshy food and a fancy smanshy drink," she says giddily.

We laugh and lean over the table, trying to find something that looks good, and I feel a tap on my shoulder. I turn my head and see Joshua towering over me.

"Hey you," he says. "How's it going?"

Still on a high from meeting Dr. East, it takes me a minute to find words. He's wearing slacks and a blazer over a dark green sweater that makes his hazel eyes look green and he's gotten a haircut since I'd last seen him. He looks like he just stepped out of a fashion magazine.

He cleans up very, very nicely, the green-eyed monster sighs, having broken out of the basement at the sight of him.

"Hey," I reply. "Good. How's everything with you?"

"It's the stalker," Lisa jokes before he can reply.

"Listen, I was personally invited to this event by the director," he retorts playfully. "But I'll take that, I'll be a stalker."

Girl, he's flirting with you!, the green-eyed monster says.

Lisa sends me a look that requires no words, mirroring the green-eyed monster's sentiments. I immediately change the subject.

"We were just looking for something good to eat, have you tried any of these?" I ask, turning back to the table laden with finger food.

Lisa has already found what she wants, smoked salmon and dill on fancy looking crackers, and she has asked the attendant for a glass of champagne.

"The salmon is good. And the oysters," he says.

I make a face expressing my dislike for oysters and respond, "I'll go with the salmon."

I put two crackers with salmon and dill on a small paper plate and select a bottle of sparkling water. Joshua grabs a bottle of sparkling water too, leaning over my shoulder to do so.

"You don't like oysters?" he asks incredulously. "Most women your age go right for the oysters or the lobster on a menu."

"Don't you mean our age?" Lisa asks rhetorically as we walk towards one of the empty tables. "And what's this about women our age? I knew you were a player."

"I am so not a player," he defends himself. "I've just been on a lot of first dates."

"I wonder why," Lisa says sarcastically.

"I just haven't found the right woman yet," Joshua says and looks over at me momentarily before opening his bottle of sparkling water.

"Enough already!" Lisa states bluntly. "How many times do I have to tell you that she's married, man?"

Both of us are used to Lisa's direct ways of speaking her mind, and fortunately, we are all able to laugh together, despite the awkwardness. The flirting is overt, and I wonder if maybe Joshua might have had a few glasses of champagne himself. He laughs but doesn't appear embarrassed by Lisa calling him out as he stutters a response.

"There's, well, there's one thing that I've learned so far in life and that is to ask for what you want. I don't ever want to make the mistake of not making myself known and then regretting it later in life," he says and takes a sip from his sparkling water.

His response is too honest and too vulnerable for Lisa to comment on, and I'm at a total loss. Lisa looks away and sips casually at her champagne. The vulnerable part of me wants to respond to the vulnerable part of him, but I know instinctively that to do so will be a catastrophic mistake. Lisa is right, I'm married, and to respond at all would be to open a door that will be impossible for me to close. I take a bite of my hors d'oeuvres and say nothing.

Joshua embodies everything that I would choose if my circumstances were different. He's kind and funny, intelligent, and compassionate, and he's active in contributing to the community, but so is Michael. The only difference is that Joshua is not a Muslim, and he's single, and Michael is Muslim, but he has taken a second wife. I have an epiphany and I realize that Joshua's presence in my life at this time is a clear sign. I'm at a crossroads. I'm being faced with an opportunity to completely change my life and it's time for me to make my choice.

Just then a pretty young woman in a close-fitting dark blue cocktail dress comes over to our table and taps Joshua on the shoulder as she smiles widely at Lisa and I. Lisa looks at me to see if I know who she is, and I discreetly shrug my shoulders. I don't know her either.

"Hey there! I thought that was you! I just wanted to come by and say hi," she says to Joshua who looks confused for a second and then recognition seems to dawn on him.

"Right. Yes. Hi," he says awkwardly and glances over at us apologetically.

In that moment I see an alternate path stretch out in front of me and I instantly, and instinctively decide that I don't want it. I already have a husband who loves me and better than that, who loves Allah. A husband who loves Allah so much that he was compelled to share that love with me by giving me a copy of the Quran and by inviting me to Islam. It doesn't get better than that and I recognize how blessed I am. As if on cue, and like a rescuing angel, Lisa responds.

"You two catch up! We have a few friends that we just have to speak to. Enjoy the lecture," Lisa says in her best imitation of a cheerful, preppy, ivy league student and grabs my arm, dragging me away before either of them can say anything.

I don't look back as we walk away, and I hold on tight to Lisa's arm.

"Thank you," I whisper gratefully as we cross the room.

"Anytime," she says and clinks her glass to my sparkling water bottle cheerily.

Chapter Eleven

Choices

"Get home safe. See you tomorrow," I say to Lisa before closing her car door.

She honks her car horn before driving off and I carefully make my way up the snow-covered driveway to the front door of my duplex. There's about 3 inches now and the snow is falling again. The night sky is a soft, dusky purple and I take my time getting my house keys from my purse to bask in the cool beauty of the falling snowflakes.

Once inside, I hang up my coat and purse on the coat rack by the door and I leave my snow-dampened high heels on the mat in front of the shoe rack. I remove my autographed copy of Race Problems and my cell phone from my purse and carry them upstairs with me. I can't help but smile thinking about the "fancy-smanshy" evening I was blessed to enjoy with my bestie.

The lecture was amazing, as expected, and I feel centered and encouraged after hearing such a clear, informative and inspirational talk about race relations in America. Contrary to what many media pundits say, race relations are still a very important topic – something that we as Americans live with everyday – so if we want to truly be able to pursue happiness we need to do the work necessary to create sincere and honest experiences with one another. Dr. Cornell East is my absolute favorite voice to listen to about these kinds of issues and I feel blessed to have been able to be in the same room with him.

I change into my warm, fleece pajamas and shake my head at myself for having made such a big deal about going earlier. Spending some one-on-one time with Lisa was just the medicine I needed and being with her helped me to see how I can do better in nurturing my friendship with Nicole. And seeing Josh again was just what I needed to get over the infatuation that had developed over the past few months.

Once in my cozy pajamas, I initiate my nighttime ritual by sitting down at the desk in the corner of the bedroom to check my emails before making my nightly duas and listening to Quranic recitation. Our old Dell creaks and buzzes as it powers up and accesses the dial-up connection through the telephone line. Soon the familiar jingle, "You've Got Mail!" greets me and I check the inbox. There are two messages from Carol about the event, and one from Joshua. My eyes widen in surprise, and I open the one from Josh first.

Hi,

I hope I didn't offend you tonight. I apologize if I did. For the record, seeing you again this summer stirred up all kinds of old feelings about you and I don't want to make the same mistake that I made in high school of not telling you how I feel. I care about you, and I really want to be a part of your life. I know you're married, and I realize that as a Muslim, it's a slippery slope to maintain a friendship with a man who is not related to you, and quite honestly, I don't just want to be your friend. I'm going out on a limb sending this and I hope your husband doesn't show up at my job ready to fight me, but it's the truth. I think you might have feelings for me too so I'm taking the chance, but even if you don't, at least you know how I feel and I can go on with my life knowing that I made myself known. I hope you reply.

Josh

I sit at the desk stunned for a few seconds and I wait to see if the green-eyed monster is going to make an appearance, but I get nothing. She's completely silent. I think this might even be a little too much for her to process. How do I respond to something like this?

I've been all over the place mentally and emotionally lately and I blame most of that on the physiological changes that my body and mind has been going through following the chemotherapy, but I take full responsibility for myself. The thought of walking a different path had been tempting, but I realize that there is nothing wrong with the path that I'm walking on, and how blessed I am. I don't want to go chasing after a fantasy that will essentially restart my whole life and possibly open up a whole new set of challenges for me to deal with, especially when God isn't at the center of it.

God had blessed me with the ability to see myself and my life for what it truly is tonight. I had buried myself so deeply into my marriage and into what I thought a Muslim woman was supposed to be that I had lost the true essence of myself. And Dr. Cornell East's lecture provided a wider context for understanding how many of us as African Americans are living the inheritance of displaced souls as descendants of slaves in this country. So much of our culture and sense of self has been lost or is unknown, and we've been battling against institutionalized racism for so long that we haven't had much time to become and to embrace our true selves.

I can also see the green-eyed monster and the broken part of me that she reflects, and I embrace her by saying: *starting tonight, I'm shedding all of the baggage in my life and focusing on solutions. This life is fleeting, beloved, and I'm not wasting one more moment doubting Allah's qadr for me.*

I close my eyes and I offer a dua to Allah: *Oh Allah, please forgive me. Oh Allah, please preserve and guide me on the straight path. Oh Allah, please dispose of my affairs towards comfort and ease.*

There's an immediate quickening in my heart and I suddenly know what I need to write back to Joshua. I click reply and begin writing.

Hi,
As salaamu alaikum,
You didn't offend me, and I apologize if I gave the impression that you had. Thank you for being so honest about your feelings and I'm very flattered. I think we both understand that it would be inappropriate for us to be friends right now. God has a plan for us all and I hope that you will discover His plan for you. My invitation for you to meet my husband is an open invitation if your feelings change.
Take good care and may Allah bless you,
As salaamu alaikum

I click send and exhale a deep, cleansing breath. Like quickfire, all of the doubts and angst that I've been feeling for the past three months disappear, and I have clarity. I've made my choice and I choose Allah, and by choosing Allah I choose myself. I choose the life and the people that I've been blessed with, with my eyes and my heart wide open, and with my spirit ready to discover what Allah has in store for the future.

I'm not naïve enough to think that everything will be easy, or that there won't be challenges or difficulties, but I hold onto the promise that with every difficulty there is relief. I get up from the desk and I cross the bedroom to the bathroom where I make wudu so I can offer two rakaats of non-obligatory prayer and my nightly duas.

All relationships have growing pains and I can clearly see now that Michael, Nicole and I have been going through our version of it. Me with the cancer and the chemo, Michael with his business and having two wives to provide for, and Nicole with her career and now a pregnancy. We've been going through these growing pains, but we haven't done a very good job empathizing with one another or with sharing the load. As a family, nothing happens to us as individuals without happening to all of us as a unit and I think we could do much better at embracing and acknowledging this. We need to embrace the fact that we are teammates. I set my heart to pray for exactly that.

I dry the water from my face, arms and feet before leaving the bathroom and returning to my bedroom to get my prayer rug. I open the curtains and the blinds to take another look at the falling snow and I leave them open so I'll be able to hear the soft, soothing patter of the snowfall as I pray. Then, I remove my prayer rug from its cubbie on my bookshelf and lay it down in front of the window, facing the east. I get a scarf from my closet, and I wrap it around my head, feeling peace like I haven't felt in a very long time. I return to the prayer rug, fold my hands over my heart, close my eyes and begin with *Allahu Akbar*.

Chapter Twelve

One Family

The next morning, I sit on my bed for almost an hour before deciding to get up and go next door to Nicole's house. I've been awake since fajr. After prayer I couldn't go back to sleep so I puttered around the house, doing laundry, loading the dishwasher, and I even dusted off the bookshelves, but it's only 9:07am now. I could call Michael I suppose, but I'd rather talk to him face to face.

Already in my sweats, I go downstairs and put on my boots before stepping out into the snow, pulling the hoodies of my sweatshirt up over my head. There's almost a foot of snow on the ground and there's another two weeks before the Thanksgiving holiday so winter is coming early this year. Gabey is going to have a ball playing in this while it lasts. With a renewed appreciation for our family, and a deep breath for courage, I walk the few steps necessary to Nicole's front door.

The bottom line is that Michael is not mine or Nicole's. He's not "mine" or "ours" any more than I/We are his. He belongs to Allah just like we belong to Allah. I belong to Allah, and I have my own choices to make, and I've made mine. We've been fortunate enough to have been brought together, to be permitted to walk together, but the choice to stay together is ours. A joint venture. We must choose to do this. And if we're true believers, we must commit to this marriage and do everything in our power to make it work. I'm finally fully and completely ready to do everything in mine.

I take a big bite of humble pie, chew completely, and swallow hard in a dry throat before knocking on the door. I hear Gabey's little voice from behind the door as he announces, "It's mommy!"

A few seconds later, Nicole opens the door with a smile.

"As salaamu alaikum, sis," she says and swings the door open wide for me to come in out of the cold.

"Walaikum as salaam," I say and step in quickly so she can close the door behind me.

Her duplex has an identical layout as mine, and she also has a small shelf on the floor below the coat rack for shoes by the door. I remove my boots and put them on the rack, remembering fondly how she and I had picked out identical shoe racks and hall tables when shopping together back in June. I'm more determined than ever to do whatever it takes to get back to a good place in our friendship. Just then Gabey runs over to me and hugs me around the legs.

"Mommy!" he says happily with a wide grin when I pick him up. "We have pancakes!"

Gabey is still wearing his footie pajamas and Nicole is wrapped up in a soft-looking turquoise bathrobe with striped socks on her feet. Her small, round baby bump protrudes from under the belt tied high around her waist.

"You do?!" I reply and kiss his sticky, syrupy face. "Can I have some?"

"Yea. A cawse," he says, and translated from Gabey-speak, he means, 'of course.'

I put him down and he holds my hand and pulls me across the living room towards the kitchen table.

Nicole follows us into the kitchen and pulls out a plate from the cabinet and says, "Michael is still sleeping. He was up late watching those Ahmed Deedat tapes. Are you coming to get Gabey?"

I put Gabey back in his booster seat so he can finish eating before sitting down at the table beside him.

"Again? He must know them by heart by now. No. I was coming to talk to Michael, but it can wait if he's still sleeping," I reply.

"Oh. Ok. Do you want some pancakes?" Nicole asks uncertainly, stopping with her hand in the air as she was about to put a second pancake on a plate for me.

"Sure. Thank you," I respond.

"How many?" she asks with a smile, and she looks happy that I've decided to stay.

"Two is good," I answer.

She brings me the plate and the maple syrup and puts them both in front of me. The atmosphere isn't as easy as it used to be between the two of us, but it's evident that we are both earnestly trying to relax and to be open with each other. Instead of focusing on difficulties that we've been having communicating, I set my heart and mind to the task of communicating better, right now, in this moment, for the sake of our friendship.

"I have to keep the syrup in the kitchen with this little old man we have here," she says conversationally, and her eyes gesture playfully to Gabey where he is boisterously eating the pancakes that she has cut up into little pieces for him.

"I know it," I respond with a smile. "He'll drench everything he eats in that stuff if I let him."

We laugh together, and Gabey looks up curiously for a second before returning his attention to the cartoon on the T.V. His presence is a unifier and I let myself imagine how much better things will be with another child in our family. There's no denying that there is something about the innocence and purity of children that makes life easier.

"Do you want some coffee or some milk?" Nicole asks me.

"Coffee would be great," I answer.

"I just made a fresh pot," she says and gets a mug from the cabinet above the counter where the coffee maker is. "And we have French vanilla flavored creamer."

She pours coffee into the mug, gets a clean spoon from the dish strainer on the counter and brings it and a dish of sugar over to me before going over to the refrigerator for the creamer.

"Thank you," I say and pour syrup on the pancakes.

"You're welcome," she replies and hands me the creamer before sitting down at the table beside Gabey and opposite me. "I'm so glad you came over. It feels like we haven't been together like this is a long time."

There's a plate of half-eaten pancakes and a cup of tea in front of her and she lifts the fork from the plate to continue eating. As she often does, she's given voice to the thought I was having, and I smile back and nod my head in agreement. The tv is on and tuned to Nick Jr. so Gabey is thoroughly enjoying himself, but I'm not feeling too bad myself. The air is comfortable between Nicole and I as we eat in silence, and I silently acknowledge Allah's grace. I try to find a conversation starter, but I get distracted when I hear Michael's footsteps coming down the stairs.

"I thought I heard your voice," he says when he reaches the bottom and sees me at the table.

He crosses the living room and joins us in the kitchen.

"Good mawning, dad," Gabey calls out through a mouthful of pancakes.

"Good morning, son," Michaels says with a sleepy grin and walks over to Gabey to kiss the top of his head.

He then leans over to hug me and says, "Good morning. As salaamu Alaikum."

"Good morning, walaikum as salaam" I reply.

The he steps around the table to Nicole and hugs her and gives her the greeting as well.

"Mmm. Pancakes," he says and takes a whiff in the air. "And coffee."

"Are you ready to eat?" Nicole asks and makes a move to get up from the table, but he places an affection, restraining hand on her shoulder.

"I can get it," he says and turns to me. "What has you up so early?"

Michael sounds surprised by my presence as he asks.

I take my time chewing the bite of pancake I had just placed in my mouth as I try to come up with a discreet explanation.

"I, uh, wanted to talk with you about something, but Nicole said you were sleeping so it can wait," I say nonchalantly.

"Is everything ok?" he asks, and I can hear the worry in his voice.

I hurry to ease his concern.

"Yes, everything is fine. It's not urgent," I reply casually.

He pours himself a cup of coffee and comes to the table to sit in the remaining empty chair.

"Do you have to go into the office today?" I ask, hoping that he doesn't.

"Later," he says and adds sugar and creamer to his coffee. "We can talk after you're done eating. Before I start getting ready."

My eyes automatically dart over to Nicole just as her eyes dart over to me. She sees my reluctance and I see her understanding.

"Our big boy is just about finished over here," she says and gets up to take Gabey's empty plate while he finishes the milk in his sippy cup. "I can take him up for a bath and get him dressed."

I smile gratefully and reply, "Thank you, sis. And I'll take him home when you're finished."

She smiles back and turns her attention to Gabriel.

"C'mon my big boy, you ready for a bath?" she asks cheerfully.

He nods his head enthusiastically and his eyes brighten.

"Bubbles!" he says when he finishes his milk.

"Yes! Bubbles! And toys! Ready to play?" Nicole asks and takes his sippy cup to place it out of his reach as she helps him out of his booster seat.

"Yea!" he answers.

She takes his hand and leads him across the living room to the staircase. Michael and I wait patiently as they climb the stairs and once we hear their footsteps fade away towards the bathroom Michael turns his full attention to me.

I'm not sure of how to begin, despite the fact that I'd spent an hour rehearsing what I wanted to tell him but now that he's in front of me I'm blank.

"What's up, babe?" he asks after watching me struggle for several seconds.

I reach for his hand and hold it in mine, taking a deep breath and exhaling slowly.

"I just wanted to talk to you about the past month and how things have been between us," I say and meet his gaze.

He's watching me and waiting as if he can't wait to hear what I have to say, as if I'm the most important person in the world to him in this moment, and I silently thank Allah for His mercy. I'm even more certain that I've made the right decision.

"I just want to say that I'm sorry for being so difficult lately. And thank you for being patient with me. It's been a struggle to figure out what I really want in life now that the cancer is gone. I had stopped looking towards the future and I didn't even realize it until recently. I'm looking now, though, and I don't know what the future holds for us, but I know that I want to spend it with you. You help me to be my best self, and I'm grateful to be blessed with you as my husband. I love you more than I can say," I tell him in one breath and I can't stop the tears that prick at my eyes when I finish.

He smiles tenderly at me and pulls me to my feet to hug me. I rest my head against his chest and inhale the fresh, sweet scent that is only his as he wraps his arms around me. We don't speak, there's no need to, and I know that everything is going to be all right between us. I don't expect the future to be easy, but I know, with faith, that there will be ease among the difficulties as we travel the roads of this life together. This is our budding little family, and I'm ready to do the best that I can to keep it strong and healthy.

Chapter Thirteen

Winter

"Don't you dare come for my pie!" Nicole tells my brother James and gives him the side eye as she deftly snatches her plate away from his fork.

We're at my parents' house for Sunday dinner the weekend before Christmas break and everyone in the immediate family has been able to make it, even Aunt Pam. We finished dinner about a half hour ago and we are sitting around in the living room getting ready to watch a movie on the VCR. Nicole is enjoying her second piece of my mother's homemade sweet potato pie and my brother James, playful as always, has tried to tease her.

"Boy don't you know you never reach for a pregnant woman's food? You'll lose your fingers!" my father jokes and everybody laughs.

Michael, Nicole, James and I don't celebrate Christmas, primarily because historically it's inaccurate in terms of celebrating Jesus' birthday, so mom has gone all out with the food spread tonight since we won't be coming over next weekend for Christmas. Her and Jasmine are upstairs getting the gifts that she bought for Gabey so he can open them. As a compromise, she promised not to use Christmas themed wrapping paper on them. My mother and Jasmine come down the stairs with arms full of gifts wrapped in solid green, red, gold and silver wrapping paper.

"Mom!" I object gently as she and Jasmine walk into the living room.

"Don't worry, it's not all for Gabey. There's something here for everybody. These are I-love-you gifts, not Christmas gifts," she says with a wink at my father as she smiles widely from ear to ear.

She sits down on the floor next to Gabey and puts all of the gifts in her arms in front of him.

"Here you go, Nana's baby," she says.

Gabriel's eyes go wide with delight, and he looks over at me as if checking for permission to rip into them.

"Don't worry about mommy, come on, Nana will help you," she says and makes a small rip in one of the boxes before handing it to him.

He promptly obeys and digs right in. Jasmine goes around the living room handing out the gifts in her arms to everyone else and Dad pops a video into the VCR.

"I get a I-love-you gift too?" James asks incredulously when Jasmine reaches him. "I hope this doesn't mean that I'm not getting any Christmas gifts. Y'all know I want that new X-Box."

He points at my mother and father to stress his point and rips into his gift.

"Oh no, my Muslim son. You don't celebrate Christmas, remember," my father says and accepts his gift from Jasmine.

"What?!" James objects and looks at my mother for confirmation.

She laughs and says, "Don't worry, son. We got you the X-Box, but you have to wait until after Christmas to get it."

"Mike, what do you have to say about this?" my father asks Michael as he accepts his gift from Jasmine and starts opening it. "He's either a Muslim or a Christian, right? As a Muslim: no pork, no alcohol, no Christmas gifts."

"Wait. Wait," James interjects and turns to Michael. "Islam is the true religion, but Christians are people of the book, right, Mike? So technically, if they're people of the book, we don't have to refuse gifts from Christians for Christmas if they want to give them to us, right?"

James and my father go back and forth playfully this way often, and Michael is usually caught in the middle. Michael's expression is dubious as he considers my brother's logic, and everyone starts laughing again.

"There's a hadeeth that says that a Muslim should never refuse a gift," Michael offers after a few thoughtful seconds.

"Good try, son" my father says.

Jasmine hands my mom her gift and then plops down beside me on the couch to hand me mine and to open hers.

"Lynne!" Aunt Pam exclaims emotionally upon opening her gift. "You guys shouldn't have! I love these!"

She holds up a pair of brand new running shoes for everybody to look at before taking off the ones she has on and replacing them.

"You're always on the run somewhere or doing something for somebody and you know your sister," my dad says. "Nothing but the best for her big sister."

"Thank you!" Jasmine exclaims next and holds up a bright purple Snuggie. "You listened!"

"Yes, we had no choice! You wouldn't stop dropping hints that you wanted one!" my mother teases.

We take turns with thank yous and showing off our gifts to one another. Nicole and I receive body wash sets, hers a sweet vanilla musk scent and mine is a citrus floral. Dad, Michael and James also get body wash and cologne, but they receive shaving kits with it. Gabey, however, is surrounded by a small sea of toys and his bright little eyes are darting back and forth between each of them, unsure of which one to play with first.

If someone would have told me six months ago that I would be sitting here in my parents' living room today, cancer free and expecting a new baby to our family, and feeling completely happy, healthy and whole, I'm sure I would have doubted her, or him.

"Thank you so much," Nicole says to my parents and sprays some of her body spray on her wrist and reaches over to let me smell it. "It smells beautiful and it's just what I like!"

Nicole and I smile at each other as I take a whiff and it's the easy, comfortable kind of exchange that I'm used to having with her, not the awkward, cautious reserve that had developed between us over the summer. We've had the chance to talk honestly and openly with each other, to cry together, and to forgive each other, and now, our friendship is stronger than ever.

"You're welcome, sweetie," my mother says and gets up from the floor to let Gabey have plenty of space to play.

The opening credits begin on the television screen and we settle down to watch. Dad turns off the ceiling light and returns to his chair, but the twinkling rainbow lights from the Christmas tree allow Gabey to see while he plays on the floor in front of it. Snow is falling beyond the wide living room windows across from where I'm sitting on the couch wedged between Jasmine and Michael, who is sitting beside Nicole, and I couldn't be more content.

My father is sitting in "his" chair, a huge, cushioned green monstrosity that he's had for years, my mother is sitting with Aunt Pam at the dining room table to the right of the living room, whispering the plot of the movie because she's already seen it, and James is in the other armchair opposite dad, shushing her. I smile and look away towards the T.V. but my gaze is caught by the falling snow.

There's a beauty in winter, particularly in falling snow, that brings a sense of peace to me that nothing else in nature can. The miracle that no snowflake is the same demonstrates some of the wonder that I feel, and I marvel at it. It's immense and magical. I peek around at our family as everyone watches the movie and I'm grateful for the miracle and uniqueness of our family. Some people may take these small, intimate moments for granted, but I see the magic in them with a deeper sense of appreciation after having come so close to death. If Allah were to call me home tomorrow, I don't believe that I would have any regrets, and this feeling is priceless. It gives me the drive to make my tomorrow even better than today, inshaa'Allah.

I lean back into the cushions of the couch and turn my eyes to the television screen, and I can't stop smiling. I think to myself, God is good, all the time, and I offer a silent thank you for these moments, hopeful that there will be many more to come.

Chapter Fourteen

Grace

"That looks beautiful! That's a perfect place for it," my mother-in-law Celeste says as she comes to stand beside me and hands me a cup of tea.

I adjust the picture frame on the center of the top shelf of the bookshelf in the living room and I smile widely. Positioned perfectly between my framed marriage certificate and my framed certificate of shahadah is our newly developed family photo. Michael is standing behind the two chairs where I'm seated on the right and Nicole is seated on the left. I'm holding a smiling Gabriel is my arms and Nicole is cradling our new addition, baby Grace, in hers.

"Michael said the photographer had to work hard to keep Gabey from reaching over to play with the baby," Celeste says.

"He sure did," I reply, and we return to the couch where we were sitting to finish organizing photographs in photo albums.

Gabriel cannot get enough of his baby sister, and he is the most adorable, doting big brother ever.

"We're over at Nicole's place more than we've been here in our own house since the baby was born," I say as I sit down. "That's his Baby Gwacie. She's all he talks about these days."

Celeste laughs as she sits down beside me and places her teacup on table.

"I've noticed," Celeste says and picks up the photo album that she was working on.

Spring is here and the trees are beginning to bud as the warm weather returns. Mama Celeste and I are putting together multiple photo albums to give as gifts with recent pictures we've developed from Nicole's baby shower and from the first visit to the hospital after the delivery. We hit the jackpot at the Dollar Tree and we were able to get six beautiful, identical photo albums: one for each of the three new grandmas and one for me, Nicole and her sister.

We're almost finished inserting the prints into the albums and we're down to the last two. Nicole is taking a nap in her place next door, but her mom, Mama Hope, and her sister Satiya have come up from South Carolina so she's not alone – not that Gabriel would ever allow such a thing. He's over at Nicole's with Michael hosting their guests and I'm sure Gabey is looking over everyone's shoulder, that is if he's even allowing anyone but him to hold his "baby Gwacie."

"You're looking good! It's hard to believe that a year ago you were diagnosed with stage four cancer. God has heard our prayers," Celeste says conversationally.

"Yes, He has," I reply with a smile. "You look great yourself. How's the non-profit doing? I can't wait to get back to New York to see the new office."

"It's going well," Celeste says and lights up at the mention of the non-profit organization that she founded for women and girls in the Bronx. "Applications for the G.E.D program came in last week and we have so many that we're going to have to arrange for two sessions this year."

"That's awesome, I'm so glad to hear it, Ma," I say. "Try not to work too hard."

"I won't," she says and takes a sip from her tea. "I'm going to enjoy my little vacation here this week and go back powered up."

"Amen to that," I say and drink some of my tea.

We finish up the photo albums, pausing every couple of minutes to gush over pictures of Grace's beautiful, tiny face. Bright sunlight streams through the windows, and I thank Allah for the blessings in my life. Polygyny certainly wasn't what I had been expecting, but now that I'm in it, I can testify that Allah is the Best of Planners. This lifestyle has tested my character and has purified my heart in ways that have caused me to love myself more than I ever have before; and loving myself has been soul changing. It's given me a brighter outlook on life, which is so important because how can I ever love others or be a positive influence in other's lives if I don't love myself?

I've come to center my life around the two greatest commandments mentioned in the Bible: Worship the Lord Your God with your whole heart, with all your soul and with all your strength; and love thy neighbor as thyself. This scripture has centered me and everything that I do is built upon this cornerstone now. Michael and I have our moments of discord and discontent, but we always come back to each other because Allah, The Eternal, The Absolute, is The One that holds us together.

The front door opens and Gabey runs in, stopping abruptly to take off his shoes, and then continues into the living room to join us. Michael comes in behind him and closes the door.

"Baby Gwacie is taking a nap," Gabriel announces and sighs. "Dad said we need to eat some lunch."

"As salaamu Alaikum," Michael says and takes off his shoes by the door before crossing the living room to sit down beside his mom on the couch.

"Walaikum as salaam," Celeste and I say in unison.

"Can I have chicken nuggets?" Gabey asks and walks into the kitchen.

"Grandma made something better than chicken nuggets," Celeste tells him, referring to herself in the third person and she gets up to follow him into the kitchen. "We have fried chicken, and baked macaroni and cheese, and fresh broccoli."

Michael rubs his stomach appreciatively and says, "I'll have some too!"

I gather up the finished photo albums and put them into the gift bags we've assembled, careful not to rip the tissue paper, and I sit back to admire them.

"Those look really nice," Michael says and wraps his arm around me. "They're going to love those."

"I hope so," I say and lean back against his chest.

In the kitchen Celeste is trying to convince Gabey to try the broccoli but he's objecting because he doesn't like the look of the chopped bell peppers and onions mixed in with it.

Celeste meets my gaze and mouths, "help" from across the room, making me and Michael laugh. Unfortunately, Gabriel is just as picky as I am when it comes to food. Michael and I get up and go into the kitchen to provide moral support to Celeste.

Gabey shakes his head no, turns his head away from Celeste's hand which is held in front of him and holding a fork with a broccoli crown on it, and says, "No. Hot."

Celeste tries to explain that these bell peppers, even though they're red, are not spicey like the red peppers that Gabey accidentally ate once on a slice of pizza, but his three-year-old mind is not convinced. Michael gives it a try and puts some broccoli into a bowl after carefully picking out all of the bell peppers and onions and then returns to Gabey.

"Try these ones, son," he says and points at the bowl. "These don't have any peppers, see?"

Gabey peers into the bowl suspiciously at first but when he doesn't see any discolorations, he accepts it and says, "Ok. Not hot?"

His bright brown eyes are wary when he asks Michael if they're hot, but he trusts him and waits for an answer.

"Nope, not hot, buddy. Try it," Michael says and sits down at the table with him.

Gabey picks a broccoli crown out with his fingers, bites it carefully and chews it hesitantly. Once he realizes that it's not hot he smiles and takes another bite.

"Not hot. It's good," he says and nods his head in acceptance.

"Let's hope Grace isn't as picky as her big brother is," Celeste says as she puts a fried chicken wing section on a plate for Gabey. "He's got a double dose of pickiness from both of you, but hopefully Grace will get more of mother's inclinations in this area than her father's."

"Hey, I'm not picky anymore," Michael objects in his own defense and they both look accusingly at me.

"I'm trying. I try. Right?" I say to both of them. "I tried those mangoes with the hot sauce on them the other day, didn't I?"

"After making a face and acting just like your son just did," Celeste says and laughs as she scoops baked macaroni and cheese onto the plate for Gabey.

"She's definitely better than she used to be," Michael says and kisses the top of my head.

Celeste makes a plate of food for Michael while I get cups and juice from the refrigerator. In the past I would have apologized for my pickiness or made an excuse for myself, but not anymore, and it's great that its ok. I've stopped second guessing myself and it's made a difference in every relationship that I have. It's been a long time since I've felt this comfortable in my own skin.

I've found my soulmate, and she is me. The green-eyed monster of my subconscious has evolved and transformed into the steady, friendly counsellor of my intuition, and I finally feel like I've discovered my purpose: family. I'm strongest when I'm with my family and supporting my family in their endeavors, just like they support me in mine. Our family has grown a little bigger now and I can only imagine what the future will hold. Family gives my life purpose, and life is good.

Shukra wal hamdulilah. Thanks and praise be to Allah.

Epilogue

25 Years Later . . . Ramadan

"Sis, do we have any more honey?" Nicole asks me as she rummages through the cabinet where we keep the sugar and all of the seasonings that we use for cooking.

"Yes, I have it over here," I say as I stir honey into my cup of chamomile tea.

I cross the kitchen to hand it to her, covering my mouth for a yawn as I go. It's 4 am and dark outside as we prepare suhoor, timing ourselves carefully so that we're not late for Fajr prayers.

"Thank you, habibty," she says sleepily, yawning by contagion after me.

"Most welcome, my sis," I reply and squeeze her shoulder affectionately, but sleepily.

We're a little greyer and a little slower waking up than we used to be, but we've been getting up together to cook breakfast before fasting during Ramadan for more than two decades now, so we've got an easy flow together as we maneuver around in the kitchen. I get started scrambling the eggs and she gets going making hash browns and boiling water for oatmeal.

"Are Gabriel and Halimah coming over this morning?" Nicole asks as she counts out potatoes for the hash browns.

Gabriel and his new bride Halimah are celebrating their first Ramadan as a married couple and have been taking the 20 minute drive over from their apartment to eat and pray fajr in congregation with the family here at our house. We've evolved from the duplex of our younger years to a two story Texas ranch style home which allows us to be close enough to each other when in need, but gives us enough space to be able to retreat when wanting a little solitude.

"Yes. They'll be here today but not tomorrow. Gabey starts work at his new job at the architect firm in the morning," I answer as I crack another egg open into the large mixing bowl.

"That's right!" Nicole says enthusiastically. "I'm so proud of that kid. He never gives up."

"Me too. I knew he had it in him," I respond. "What about Gracie, Dillon and the baby? Are they coming over?"

"Not for suhoor. Gracie going to trying cooking herself today! But they'll be here for iftar to break fast later," Nicole says.

Grace and her husband Dillon live a few streets over and have a baby girl named Safiyah.

"Ok. Good for her! She's had enough practice over the years, I'm sure she'll make us proud. She's another one who never ceases to amaze me. All of our kids have turned out all right, I must say. Subhanaa'Allah," I reply.

"Subhanaa'Allah," Nicole repeats. "Speaking of which, Atiyaa should be up here by now. That girl must have fallen back to sleep."

"You know she did," I say and we laugh together.

Atiyaa is Nicole and Michael's fifteen-year-old daughter. After the cancer and the chemotherapy, I was never blessed with anymore children, but Nicole and Michael had had two more. Musa, their sixteen-year-old, was also most likely fast asleep in his bedroom although he was known to surprise us by getting up early before anyone else during Ramadan to pray non-obligatory prayers throughout the night.

My iphone pings with a text message so I pause with the eggs and pick it up from the counter to check it. It's from my brother James. He has sent a picture of him and Joshua standing in front of Al Azhar mosque in Egypt.

James and Joshua are celebrating Ramadan in Egypt this year with the community basketball team that they coach. The team is competing in an international basketball tournament there. Joshua took his shahadah with James at a local masjid in RI back in the day and they've been close friends ever since.

"Wow! Look at this!" I say to Nicole and walk over to the stove to show her the picture on my phone.

She looks up from peeling potatoes and gazes at the photo.

"Wow!" she says. "That's so awesome. I know James must be loving it there."

"I know," I agree as my phone pings with three more pictures.

We scroll through them together, oohing and ahhing at the beauty and majesty of the architecture. Atiyaa comes into the kitchen as were looking.

"What's that?" she asks and stands behind us, leaning against our shoulders to peer down at the pictures. "Look at Uncle James! He's in Egypt, right?"

"Um-hm," I reply and scroll back to the top so she can see all of the photos.

"Where's your brother?" Nicole asks Atiyaa and goes back to peeling potatoes.

"Sleeping," she answers. "You know how hard he is to wake up. He wouldn't budge."

"That's ok. Let him sleep. He only rushes us anyway and isn't much help," Nicole says.

"What can I do?" Atiyaa asks us.

"You can cut up the fruit," I say and point to the melon and cantaloupe on the island in the center of the kitchen.

"Ok," she says and goes over to the sink to wash her hands.

"Are Lisa and everybody going to make it here next weekend?" Nicole asks me.

"Looks like it," I say with a jolt of energy at the thought of them coming to visit us in Texas. "I can't believe it's been ten years since we last saw each other! I can't wait to see them and hug them!"

"And to cry, I'm sure," Nicole says with a sweet smile. "You've always been a softy, but you've gotten even more sentimental with age.

We laugh at that, but my eyes get watery just thinking about seeing Lisa, Amelia and Ellie again after so many years apart. Lisa and Amelia are still living in RI with their families, both of them now married with kids too, but Ellie and I have both moved out of state with our husbands and children.

"I know it. Can't deny it a bit. I can hardly watch a hallmark commercial without getting weepy," I reply as I stir the scrambled eggs.

"Before you know it, you'll be playing bingo and starting book clubs like your Aunt Pam," Nicole teases.

I laugh and reply, "And you'll be right there with me! I see you getting teary at those commercial too!"

"You're so right, TiTi," Atiyaa agrees adamantly. "She was just crying over some corny commercial last night!"

We laugh together and get down to the business of preparing breakfast. Atiyaa gets started cutting up the fruit into bite sized chunks and Nicole begins slicing the peeled potatoes into chips for homestyle homefries with onions. I season the dozen eggs I've cracked and thoroughly mix them in the mixing bowl before seeking out the large frying pan for scrambling them. We've got the whole process

down to a science and 40 minutes later we've set
the table, poured cups of orange juice, set out
bottles of spring water, and we are carrying platters
of eggs, hash browns, fruit and toast to the dining
room table.

Gabey and Halimah arrive just as Michael and
Musa come upstairs to the dining room.

"Good morning and as salaamu alaikum, family,"
Gabey calls out as he shuts the front door behind his
new bride.

"Gabe!" Musa cries, suddenly wide awake and
excited to see his older brother.

"Whatsup, Mu. Hey everybody," he says once he
and Halimah have climbed the stairs and crossed the
living room to get to us.

We exchange hugs and salaams eagerly, as if we
hadn't all just seen each other the day before. My
heart is so full I can't stop smiling.

"Smells good," Michael says once we're all seated
around the table. "Shall we?"

That's family code speak for let's say the blessing
and dig in. We lift our hands in dua while Michael
offers the prayer:

Oh, Allah. We thank you for this food that we are about to receive, and for all of your many blessings. Amin.

We all say "amin" in unison and smile happily as we begin making our plates. I thank Allah for another year of fasting, for another year with family, and for another opportunity to strive towards the good.

Glossary

Abaya: a traditional, loose, robe-like dress worn by many Muslim women

Al Azhar: one of the most important mosques and Islamic universities in the world

Al hamdulilah: an Arabic phrase of praise meaning All Praise is to Allah (God)

Allah: the Arabic word for God

Allahu Akbar: an Arabic phrase meaning God is The Greatest

As salaamu alaikum: The Muslim greeting commonly translated as meaning peace be upon you

Asr: The middle afternoon required Islamic salaat prayer

Astagfirullah: The Arabic phrase meaning Allah, forgive me

Dawah: the act of inviting people to embrace, or convert to, Islam

Deen: the way of life of Muslim believers which complies with the divine laws, beliefs and deeds associated with the Islamic religion

Dhikr: a form of Islamic meditation in which phrases or prayers are repeatedly chanted to remember God

Dua: Prayer supplications; can be made at any time of the day and does not require the ritual cleansing of Wudu to be offered

Fajr: The pre-dawn required Islamic salaat prayer

Fard: that which is required by Islamic law according to the religion of Islam

Habibty: the Arabic feminine word for beloved or sweetheart

Hadeeth: teachings of the sayings and sunnah of the Prophet Muhammad (may peace be upon him)

Hijab: a veil worn by many Muslim women in the presence of any male outside of their immediate family which covers the hair, head and chest.

Hijab pin: a small pin used by Muslim women for securing a scarf or khimar

Imam: the title of the religious leader of the mosque/masjid in the Islamic religion

Inshaa'Allah: an Arabic term meaning if God wills or if God permits

Isha: the nightly required Islamic salaat prayer

Salat al-Istikaarah: the prayer of seeking council recited by Muslims who are in need of guidance from God when facing a decision in their life

Jumuah: The Friday congregational prayer at the Masjid/Mosque practiced by Muslims

Khimar: a hijab veil worn by Muslim women

Kufi: a brimless, short, rounded cap worn by some Muslim men and among many populations in Africa and Southern Asia

Masha'Allah: an Arabic phrase in the form of praise meaning "this is what God wills"

Masjid/Mosque: consecrated prayer space for worship in the Islamic community

Polygyny: the Islamic tradition of marriage between one man and up to a maximum of four women

Qari: a person in the Islamic tradition who has memorized and recites the Quran with the proper rules of recitation

Quran: The holy revelation of the Islamic religion as revealed to the Prophet Muhammad (peace be upon him) by the Archangel Gabriel 1400 years ago

Rakaats: a cycle of prescribed movements and prayers that are performed in the ritual Islamic salaat

Ramadan: an Islamic holiday celebrating the revelation of the Holy Quran which includes 30 days of fasting from sunrise to sunset

Salaams: a casual term referring to greeting someone with the Islamic greeting of peace

Salaat: The required ritual Islamic prayer taught by the Prophet Muhammad (may peace be upon him) to be prayed at five specific times daily by all Muslims; Fajr, Zuhr, Asr, Maghrib, and Isha

Shahadah: One of the major tenets of belief in Islam and the Muslim declaration of faith; La ilaha ilalah (There is no God but Allah)

Shalwar kameez: a traditional combination dress worn by women, and in some regions by men in South Asia which are typically trousers and a long shirt or tunic.

Shukra wal hamdulilah: an Arabic phrase meaning thanks and praise be to Allah.

Subhaana'Allah: an Arabic phrase meaning glory to God

Surahs: the Arabic word loosely translated to mean chapters which refers to the chapters of the Quran

Taqwa: an Islamic term for being conscious and cognizant of God, of truth and of piety

Walaikum as salaam/Wasalaamu alaikum: The Muslim response to the greeting of As Salaamu Alaikum and commonly translated as meaning and peace be returned to you

Wudu: The ritual cleansing for the Islamic ritual salaat prayer

Two Wives, One Family

Music Playlist

Chapter One, Summer: Weather – Amel Larrieux

Chapter Two, Home: Overjoyed – Stevie Wonder

Chapter Three, Back to Life: Get Up – Amel Larrieux

Chapter Four, Adulthood: Say – John Mayer

Chapter Five, Change: Speak to My Heart – Donnie McClurkin

Chapter Six, The Green-Eyed Monster: Hide Me – Kirk Franklin

Chapter Seven, Heartbreak: Can't Give Up Now – Mary Mary

Chapter Eight, Searching for Meaning: Didn't Cha Know – Erykah Badu

Chapter Nine, Meltdown: Even If – Amel Larrieux

Chapter Ten, Temptation: In Love With You – Erykah Badu

Chapter Eleven, Choices: Times 'A Wastin' – Erykah Badu

Chapter Twelve, One Family: For Real – Amel Larrieux

Chapter Thirteen, Winter: A Closer Walk With Thee – Fred Hammond

Chapter Fourteen, Grace: Sent from Heaven – Keyshia Cole

About the Author

Janette Grant is an author and the Owner and Executive Editor of Mindworks Publishing, a desktop publishing company specializing in the production of books that build interfaith bridges for promoting understanding and tolerance between cultures.

She is a convert from Christianity to Islam and she has a deep personal interest in interfaith discussions. She writes poetry in her free time, and she currently resides outside of Houston, Texas with her family.

You can follow her on social media by searching:

Mindworks Publishing and Janette Grant on Facebook and Instagram